No Problem, We'll Fix It

Lyle Weis

To Susan,
Who is helping
writers do what they
want!
Lyle

To Donna, Erica and Jared, who kept the book warm

A JUNIOR GEMINI BOOK

Published in 1991 by
General Paperbacks
30 Lesmill Road
Toronto, Canada
M3B 2T6

Canadian Cataloguing in Publication Data

Weis, Lyle Percy
No problem, we'll fix it

"Junior Gemini"
ISBN 0-7736-7297-4

I. Title

PS8595.E578N6 1991 jC813'.54 C91-093829-6
PZ7.BZ7.W457No 1991

Cover Illustration: June Lawrason
Typesetting: Tony Gordon Ltd.

Printed and bound in the United States of America

CHAPTER ONE

Have you ever wished for something bad to happen — then it actually does? Well, if you have, you know how I felt when my mom and I were driving to my cousins' place and our tire blew. Only seconds earlier I had been thinking, Oh, please, let the car break down. Or let us get there and find they've gone to Argentina or someplace. Anything, because I *don't* want to go!

And just like that, *fwoompp*! Followed by a loud *thumpa, thumpa, thumpa* from someplace on the car. I couldn't believe my ears. Did I — an average twelve-year-old girl — suddenly have supernatural powers?

"What was *that*?" my mother asked as she hit the brakes.

"How am I supposed to know?" Boy, was I scared there for a second. I mean, it seemed too weird. Then I began to feel pretty good: my prayers had been answered.

Mom steered toward the shoulder of the gravel road, and the car shuddered to a halt. Dust, stirred up behind us, drifted out over a field where some green plants were growing. Back in Edmonton I would have called it tall grass, but here I was sure the farmers referred to it as wheat or barley or another kind of crop. I didn't really care. I just wanted to go back to the city.

Mom got out, walked from the driver's side to the back of the car and then came up along my side. She bent down, put her hands on her hips and made a face. "Kim, you might as well get out."

I opened the door and stood beside her. The front tire was flat. No, not simply flat. It was squished and mangled looking. There we were, absolutely in the middle of nowhere, with no telephone, no houses in sight and a tire that looked like a pancake I'd tried to make once.

"Darn," I said, trying to keep from smiling. "Guess this means we'll have to cancel our plans." I emphasized the word *our*.

"Don't be silly, we're almost there. Besides, it's only a flat tire."

"Mom," I said a little impatiently, "what are we going to do? We haven't passed another car for almost ten minutes, and absolutely nobody lives around here."

"Oh, lots of families live nearby. There

are farms all around us." She swept her arm in a half-circle.

All I saw was miles and miles of green nothing. Not a single building or one person. A little farther along was a bridge that crossed a ravine or small valley.

"What will we do?" she repeated. "Well, we're just going to change the tire, that's what."

I groaned. Ever since she and Dad separated last fall and we moved from Toronto to Edmonton, Mom has insisted on "doing things" she's never done before.

Like the time the bathroom sink clogged up at our place.

I came home from school to find Mom on her back, her head stuck inside the cupboard, and she was using the kind of language she's always on my case for using. Mom's a nurse, and the kind of tools she understands are thermometers. Well, the tool kit Dad had left behind was open beside her, and wrenches were scattered all over.

Oh, sure, she fixed the clog. After about three hours. But there was black gunk all over the place. And guess who had to help her clean it up? If she had asked my opinion, I would have told her she was just trying to prove something by "doing things" herself. Of course, she never asked me. And I didn't think that was fair.

"Mom, I told you this was a bad idea. I mean, this is no ordinary flat tire — it — it's an omen!" Sure, I was laying it on a bit thick, but I figured I had nothing to lose.

"Don't be silly." She put the key in the trunk lock, and the lid popped open. As she reached in and grabbed a suitcase, she talked to me over her shoulder.

"We need a break from each other. We've been getting on each other's nerves ever since —" She paused, avoiding mentioning my dad. "For the past few months."

"That's not the *only* reason," I said darkly. "You want me out of the way so you can spend more time alone with what's-his-name . . . Alvin."

"That's *Allan*."

I knew his name, all right. She had started going out with him — one of our neighbors — a few weeks earlier. I didn't like the guy. He was too smooth. And she was mushy around him, the way she never had been around Dad.

"He has nothing to do with it, Kim! Why won't these stupid things move?" She grunted and straightened up, forgetting that she was standing under the raised lid. Her head made a hollow *bonk* as it hit the lid. "Ow, damn!" She backed up carefully, rubbing a spot above her ear. Though she forced a smile, her face was red and I knew she was mad at me.

"All right, yes. I will be seeing Al. But I would even if you were at home, don't you see? Come on, this proves we need a little breathing space. Two weeks at the farm with your cousins will do you a lot of good. You can go horseback riding, and the Tyrrell Museum in Drumheller, where they have the dinosaur exhibits, is only a short drive away. Oh, just wait, you'll love it!"

That got to me. You see, I had a feeling I *would* like seeing my cousins, especially Valerie, who was the same age as me. We'd had a great time several years ago when we'd last gotten together. But I didn't like the fact that Mom seemed to think she had to have me out of the way for a while. And, maybe, Drumheller wouldn't have been so bad if it wasn't almost a whole day's drive south of Edmonton.

"You don't really care if I'll love it or not." I turned around, crossed the wide ditch and sat down on the ground.

Mom stared at me for a moment, then slowly went back to pulling things out of the trunk. At last she came up with the spare tire, and heaved it over the edge of the trunk opening.

She grunted, so I knew it must have been

pretty heavy. Mom is not a big woman — she always buys her dresses in the petites section of the clothing stores. Part of me wanted to jump up and help her. We always do the chores around the house together, so I didn't feel right not helping her now.

The tire flipped, hit the bumper and bounced to the ground. Mom gave chase as it rolled toward the ditch, then she tried to jump in front of it to head it off. She tripped, landed on her bum, and the tire rolled between her legs and thumped her in the chest before stopping. I couldn't help giggling.

She gave me a long look, wrestled the tire up the slope and leaned it against the car. I guess things could have been worse. I mean, at least the *spare* wasn't flat, too! Next she took from the trunk a weird-looking thing with a big screw in the middle, and a flat gray metal tool case. I was beginning to hate the sight of tool cases.

A strange feeling came over me then. I saw Mom next to our little car, looking almost as if she were all alone on that deserted dirt road under a huge blue Alberta sky. I could feel my anger slipping out of my body.

I got to my feet, crossed the ditch and stood behind her. "Could I, uh, help?"

She turned. Her face did a gradual change, slipping into a smile. One thing about Mom: she never stays upset with me for long.

"Help is exactly what I need," she said. "Now then," she went on, holding up the thing with the screw through its middle. "This, I think, is the jack. See, the picture shows how you put it under the car." She pointed to arrows in an outline drawing of our Toyota.

"Uh, Mom, have you ever done this before?"

"No."

"Thought so." I walked to the passenger door.

"Where are you going?" she asked.

"To get the first-aid box in the glove compartment. We're going to need it before this is over."

She laughed, and it was good to see her happy again.

"Very funny. Just give me a hand here," she told me.

I pried off the hubcap with a screwdriver — and skinned my knuckle — while she began cranking up the jack. As she turned the crank, the legs of the jack came closer together and the car began to rise.

"Hey, it works!" she cried.

I had to admit that it did. Just the same, I kept an eye on the car in case it started to fall off the jack.

Next she used a wrench to loosen the nuts on the wheel. But every time she gave a tug, the wheel spun a little. The nuts, however, stayed tight.

"This can't be right," she said. "Kim, hold the tire still, okay?"

Even though I wrapped my arms around the wheel in a bear hug and she tried to squeeze the wrench in past my ribs, the tire still moved. My head flopped around like a rag doll's.

Finally we lowered the car until the tire just touched the ground. The wheel didn't turn any more, and we got it off. We lifted the spare up, and while I held it in place, Mom spun the nuts on by hand. She turned the crank down again until the rubber touched the ground, and I used the wrench to tighten the nuts.

Mom hummed as she took the wrench and gave each nut a final twist. It was the same dumb old song she always hummed or sang when she felt good. Something about "Blue skies smilin' on me . . ." Well, there were sure plenty of those out there. Blue, big and empty.

I was beaten, and knew it. She was putting on that wide grin of hers, the one she had when she said, "Oh, sure, we can fix the sink," or "Oh, sure, we can change a tire." Trouble was, sometimes she was right.

I decided to try one more angle — though it was weak.

"What about Ruffles?" I asked. Ruffles is my dog, a warm, lovable basset hound who hates to be alone. "You'll be at work all day. Who will feed him and keep him company?"

"Ruffles will survive — and so will you." She gave me a squeeze, then began to laugh, pointing to me, then herself. My blouse and jeans were covered in dirt; her face and arms were grimy.

Great, I thought. I'm about to spend two weeks in the middle of nowhere with people I hardly know. Nothing ever happens in a place like this. People are probably so bored they get excited when a gopher or a bird goes by. I sighed and was about to pull the jack from under the car, when a big shadow passed overhead. At the same time, the air whispered briefly. I glanced up just as a large bird settled on a fence post across the road from us.

"Mom, look!"

"Some kind of a hawk, I think. Beautiful, isn't it?"

As we stared at it, the bird seemed to stare right back at us. It looked almost two feet long to the tip of its tail, and had a black head, with a kind of mustache marking behind its beak. The chest was white, but the wings and tail were a bluish black, almost like the head. It *was* beautiful, so graceful looking, yet proud and strong, too.

"Somewhere I think I've seen — " I began, then stopped. I recognized the bird, and it wasn't an ordinary hawk. I got up slowly and opened the car door. Reaching into the back seat, I found my camera, the one my dad had given me for Christmas.

"What are you doing, Kim?"

"I think that's a peregrine falcon, Mom! It would be great if I could get a picture of it."

"Are you sure?"

Sometimes Mom and I are not on the same wavelength. It's as if our minds are seeing things from different places. It happened then. I nearly got mad at her. "Of course it would be great! Hardly anyone gets to see one of these falcons up close, and to get a picture of your own . . . I bet I could even sell it to a newspaper. Come *on*, Mom!"

"No, no," she said patiently. "I mean, is it really a peregrine? They're supposed to be almost extinct, aren't they?"

"Oh." I almost felt like apologizing to her. Instead I muttered, "Uh, yeah, there're only a few hundred left in the world. And

I'm positive this is one of them. Look at the markings on the head. 'Scuse me." I squeezed by her and leaned over the hood of the car to steady the camera. The falcon perched rock still, almost as if he knew what I wanted and was waiting for me. I took a deep breath, held it and pressed the button.

Just then we heard someone coming along the road, and I turned to see a green pickup slow down after cresting a small rise behind us. As the driver pulled off the road and stopped a short distance from us, the red, white and blue lights on the middle of its roof began flashing. When the driver got out, I saw he wore a uniform. A second man stayed seated in the truck.

"Mom," I whispered out of the corner of my mouth, "remember what I said about a bad omen?"

CHAPTER TWO

The uniformed man walked up to our car, but he kept glancing across the road at the bird, which still perched on the fence. When he spoke, his voice wasn't very friendly.

"You folks got a problem?"

My mom backed up a little. "Well, uh, yes, as a matter of fact. We have a flat tire." She pointed to the jack and the ruined tire on the ground.

He stepped around to get a better look. He was wearing sunglasses, which he pushed up onto his forehead for a second, before lowering them again. His hair, very black and wavy, curled over his ears, and as he turned to me, he ran his fingers through it once.

"You were taking pictures." His tone wasn't at all friendly, more like he was accusing me of something.

"Well, yeah. Is there something wrong with that?"

The mirrored sunglasses only stared at me for a moment. "No. Not with pictures." He touched the hair over his ear again. "If the tire's fixed, I suppose you'll be on your way soon."

Out of the corner of my eye I saw the passenger door of the truck open and the other man get out. He began walking toward us as Mom put her hand on my shoulder and started chewing out the man with the wavy hair.

"What is this?" she said angrily. "We run into trouble out here, and we get the third degree. Who are you people, anyway?"

"We're with the Department of Fish and Wildlife," the second man said as he walked up to join us. He seemed a bit older than the other one, maybe Mom's age or even more. "Is there some problem, Bob?" he asked the first man.

"Maybe not," Bob answered, and circled around our car for a better look at the falcon.

He stood with his back to us, his arms crossed on his chest. I had a feeling that he knew we were watching him, because he seemed to be putting on an act.

"This is ridiculous," my mother said.

I recognized the tone in her voice. It was the one she used when she thought she had told me too many times that my room was a total disaster. Her temper builds and builds like lava in a volcano before it finally erupts. "We haven't done anything wrong, yet we're being treated like suspects in a crime. I demand to know what the problem is."

The second officer nodded. "Yes. You're right. It's just that we —" He turned to include the one called Bob, who was now walking back to the truck, ignoring us.

The officer talking to us stared at him. "Look," he said, "my partner there, Bob, is still kind of new — he's been on the job for less than a year — and he's eager to do his best. Sometimes he overreacts. I'm very sorry if we've upset you."

He sounded as if he truly meant it. He wasn't wearing sunglasses, and I can usually tell by looking into a person's eyes if he's lying or telling the truth. His eyes were a bright blue, and looked great against his suntanned face. His forehead was lined, as if he worried a lot, yet he looked like a kind man.

My mother's face softened. She wasn't going to erupt this time.

"Well," she said, "that's all right. Maybe I flew off the handle, too. It's a hot day, and we've been driving for a while."

"Where are you from?"

"Edmonton. We're visiting family near Drumheller."

"Oh. That's . . . nice."

The two of them smiled and there was an awkward silence.

Mom looked away for a moment. "We took the shortcut through a town called Rosebud, and now, if we're on the right track, we're looking for Road 569."

"You're doing fine. Five-sixty-nine is across that bridge, another couple of kilometers."

He had a nice voice, as though he wanted to make sure we weren't worried or anything. He sure was being nice to my mother.

I decided to interrupt. "My mom and I were having an argument when you came along. I say that bird is a peregrine falcon, and she doesn't believe me."

"Kim! We were not arguing — I simply wasn't sure." She shot me a glance that said "What are you up to?" before shrugging and smiling again at the officer.

"Yes, you've got a good eye, young lady. That is indeed a peregrine."

"I knew it," I blurted. "I saw one last year when our class took a field trip to the building in Edmonton where it has a nest, and we watched it on closed-circuit television!"

"Right. This male is one of the few left in Alberta. He belongs to an endangered species. We've been trying to keep an eye on that falcon for some time now, but it's not easy, because we have such a large area to cover."

He paused, looking from my mother to me and back again. "I guess we owe it to you to say that we've had trouble recently in the district with people stealing eggs and young birds from nests."

"Why would anyone do such a thing?" my mother demanded.

Sometimes Mom surprises me by what she doesn't know. "Mr. Roskey, our science teacher," I broke in, "said that sometimes people steal the young birds and smuggle them out of the country. In places like Saudi Arabia and Europe, rich people train them and keep them as hunters. They're worth a lot of money."

"That's right," the officer said. "And occasionally somebody will shoot one, just to have it stuffed for a mantel. Crazy, isn't it? But our biggest problem right now is the one your daughter mentioned." He paused before extending his hand. "I should introduce myself. Name's Paul Tessier."

My mother shook his hand. "I'm Teresa Hall. This is my daughter, Kimberley."

For some reason, Mom uses the long version of my name when she introduces me, even though she knows I hate it. Makes me sound like some rich snot who dresses in bows and frilly blouses. Yuck.

"Do you believe us," she was asking, "when we say we're not smugglers or poachers?"

Mr. Tessier's face creased in a big grin. It was amazing to me how easy it was to talk to him, even though we had known him for only a few minutes. He raised his eyes to look at Mom and she glanced over at the falcon, which still perched motionless.

Suddenly I felt a little out of place. I guess Mom is pretty — I don't really know. But there was a look in the officer's eyes that I've seen before, and it made me feel funny inside. I mean, I liked him, but I felt uncomfortable all the same. I coughed and looked at my watch.

Mr. Tessier cast a glance at his truck. "Well, if you people are sure you can manage, I'll leave you to it. I'll wait, though, just to make sure you're safely away."

"Thanks, we're almost done."

It took us only a while longer to get the jack and luggage back in the trunk. When Mom started the engine, the falcon finally took off, using long easy strokes of his wings to lift himself upward.

I turned around in the seat to watch the truck pull a U-ey in the road. "Would you say he's handsome?" I asked.

Picking up her sunglasses from the dashboard and putting them on, she replied, "Sort of. Then again, uniforms help make men look impressive."

I wasn't so sure about that. Mom's friend Al was a salesman who wore a suit to work. A business suit was sort of a uniform, and I thought he looked boring.

"He had nice eyes," I said.

"Yes, he —" She stopped herself and reached over to tap a book of mine on the dashboard. "What are you reading now?" she asked.

"*The Sword in the Stone*." I reached out for the paperback. "I've read it before. A couple of times. It's about King Arthur when he was a boy."

"Must be good if you're reading it for the third time."

"Yeah."

I liked Arthur, whose nickname in the book is Wart. His friend Merlyn the Magician changes Wart into all sorts of things, including a hawk. I sure could have used a magician at that moment. Someone who could transform me into a powerful peregrine, maybe, so I could soar off whenever I wanted. Instead I was trapped in a car like some prisoner going off to jail.

We crossed the bridge ahead, which straddled a river. It was a long bridge, because the river twisted and turned. Mom told me to look out the window. The fields were probably growing wheat, she said. I yawned.

"If I remember correctly," she told me, "we're only about a mile from the farm." The road climbed a gradual slope, and when we topped that, a gathering of buildings stood quite a way back from the road. "Yes, there they are!"

As we turned from the gravel into the dirt drive, I read the black lettering on a gray mailbox: J. Schultz.

The driveway went on for hundreds of feet, past a wire fence behind which some cows stared at us, before coming to an end in front of a big white house. Off to one side was a red barn, and between the house and barn was a square building that looked like a garage or shed. As we got out of the car, I heard yelling coming from behind the garage. Pretty soon a kid younger than me, maybe nine or so, came ripping around the side of the garage toward us, giggling and running like crazy. A second later a girl about my age came after him in hot pursuit.

"If I lay my hands on you, I'll rip your ears off!" she screamed.

Neither one of them really seemed to notice us. As she churned after him around our car, I saw that her hair and face were wet and her dark blue T-shirt was stuck to her back. They stopped on opposite sides of the car, the boy beside my mother, the girl by me. He giggled once more and pushed his glasses farther up on his stubby nose.

From inside the house a woman cried out, "What are you two up to now?" The back screen door opened, and my aunt appeared. "Why can't you two get — Oh! Look who's finally here!"

My aunt reminds me a lot of my mother — which isn't strange, I guess, since they are sisters. They both have dark hair and blue eyes, and they both laugh a lot. Sometimes it gets to you. Like then.

She came down the stairs, laughing at nothing that I could see, except maybe her kids having acted like a couple of maniacs a minute earlier. She hugged my mom, then me, then stopped dead to stare at my cousin beside me. "Valerie! You're absolutely dripping!"

Valerie said through clenched teeth, "I *know,* Mother, and there's the little creep who did it! He sprayed me with the hose!"

"Jason, please don't pester your sister." My aunt tried, but couldn't quite make a frown. She turned to my mother and me. "You must be dying of thirst, driving on a hot day like this! Come in. It's almost time for supper. I was beginning to think you weren't going to make it."

My aunt leading the way and my mother explaining about the flat tire, we climbed the porch stairs to go inside. On the way I heard Valerie behind me say, "You're not getting away with this, twerp. I'll get even."

We had some lemonade before sitting down to eat. My Uncle John came in and said hello. He wasn't at all like my aunt; he spoke very quietly and, instead of kissing my mom hello or hugging her, just shook her hand and smiled. His face and hands were tanned the darkest brown you could imagine. We sat down to eat around a big table in a kitchen that was as large as our living room at home.

"So, Kimberley," my aunt said while passing around a huge bowl of mashed potatoes, "you certainly have shot up!"

"Guess so." I shrugged. "Uh, could you just call me Kim? I like it better."

"Well, yes, of course. Kim."

Surprise showed in her eyes as she looked from me to Mom and back. Mom at least had the sense not to say something sarcastic.

"Well," my aunt continued, "the last time we saw you was when we went to Toronto back — when was that, John, four years ago?"

My uncle nodded. He was busy dishing out some peas in the pod.

I suddenly realized how hungry I was and took three scoops of mashed potatoes and bathed them with gravy.

"Don't these girls look alike now, Teresa? I mean, of course, except for the hair."

Valerie's hair is blond, with a natural wave, whereas mine is a dark brown and straight as uncooked spaghetti. My aunt looked at me, then at Valerie, who grinned across the table at me and rolled her eyes.

My uncle, as I said, is kind of quiet. The only time he spoke during dinner was when he asked how our drive had been.

"Fine, except we got a flat tire," my mother answered. "But Kim and I fixed it. No problem."

She sounded proud when she said that, and the funny thing was, I felt a little proud myself when she described what we had done.

"Oh," I added, "and we almost got arrested."

"What!" My aunt's mouth made a perfect O shape and hung open.

"We did *not* almost get arrested." Mom corrected me, but gently, as if she didn't mind the kidding. Then she described our meeting with the officers from Fish and Wildlife.

Jason listened closely, his elbows on the table, his chin in his hands. "How much are those kings and princes willing to pay for the falcons?" he asked.

"Something I read said as much as $20,000," I answered.

"Wow! A guy could get rich!" His eyes grew round and greedy.

"Sure, right," I said, not making any effort to keep the anger out of my voice. "That's why they're almost extinct." After a second I added, "And they take the young ones out of the nest, away from their parents. How would you like that?"

There was silence around the table. My uncle coughed into his hand and said, "Excuse me, Kim, could you pass the gravy?"

Jason's face was red. "Uh, are you sure the bird you saw was a peregrine falcon?" he finally asked. "What did it look like?"

Mom told him, leaving out the most important detail, the mustache marking on its head, which I supplied. Jason and his sister exchanged quick sideways glances, but said nothing. Nobody else at the table noticed except me, and I wondered what secret they were sharing.

All through the rest of the meal, Jason kept staring at me. I ignored him at first, then stared back. When that didn't make him stop, I waited until no one else was looking, then crossed my eyes and touched the tip of my nose with my tongue. Not many people can do that, believe me. Jason's eyes bugged out, and he finished eating by gazing into his plate.

Afterward, while the adults sat around the table talking, Valerie came into the living room and asked me, "Go for a walk?"

I shrugged. Might as well, since I had already checked the television; they didn't have cable or a satellite dish like some farms we had passed, so there would be no MuchMusic for the next two weeks. I already missed civilization.

On the way out, I stopped by the coat hooks near the kitchen door for my sweater and my camera, which was hanging by its strap.

My uncle looked up. "Pretty nice camera, Kim. Yours?"

"Yeah. Dad gave it to me for Christmas." I felt my face get hot. I remembered what my father had told me over the phone about the gift, how he hoped I would send lots of pictures of myself. " 'Bye," I said hurriedly, and followed Valerie.

Outside, we crossed the dirt yard on the way to the barn. "I'm glad you came," said Valerie. "Weekends and holidays can get a little long and lonely sometimes." She glanced over her shoulder. "Beat it, Jason!"

Her brother was following us — at a safe distance.

"Don't you have any neighbors?"

"Oh, sure. I have a friend who lives about a kilometer away. I visit her sometimes on my bike. And I see friends in town, too. But still . . ." She laughed. "It's nice to have someone new!"

"Yeah, guess so." It sounded to me as if the farm was like an island. Just as I'd thought.

Inside the barn, it was cool and sort of dark. Valerie showed me a saddle on a bench and asked me if I liked horseback riding. I didn't want to admit to her I'd been on a horse only once in my life, so I said it was all right every once in a while. We took a small door out the back of the barn and cut through a field toward some cows. I was staring up, watching the sun lower itself in the sky and thinking I might get a good sunset photo, when Valerie grabbed my elbow.

"Watch out!"

I stopped and looked down. My runner, my new white Reebok, was sinking in a greenish brown slime. "Yuck!" I pulled my foot up slowly, and that's when the smell hit me and I knew what it was: cow pie, fresh, gooey and stinking for all it was worth.

Behind us I could hear laughter — a high, giggly *he-he-he*, which I had already heard once that day. I turned to see Jason, doubled up, holding his sides and guffawing like an idiot.

"Just ignore him," said Valerie. "Get lost!" she yelled, while giving me a steadying arm to hang on to. Then she dug into her back pocket and brought out a tissue. "Here, try wiping it off with this."

I did, and managed to get some on my fingers and pants before I was finished. Under my breath I used a few choice curses for the animal that had laid that prize in my path.

"Hey, Kim, way to go!" Jason mimicked me by taking giant steps, then stopping abruptly to look down at his foot with a horrified expression. "Oh, no. Poo on my shoe!"

I shook my fist at him and started in his direction, but Valerie grabbed me. "Wait, I've got something planned for him," she whispered. To her brother she said, "Jason, if you leave us alone for a little while, I'll let you have my share of cake tonight."

He turned and ran back toward the house.

With a sly grin, Valerie told me, "Come on, let's go down to the pond."

That evening before going to bed, we all

gathered again in the kitchen. The adults had tea and we had milk and cake. Valerie had a nibble of hers, then said she wasn't hungry and offered it to Jason. He happily gobbled the second piece along with his own. Mom pulled out the sofa bed in the living room, and I helped Valerie set up a cot in her room for me. We changed fast, then waited quietly so we could hear Jason in the room next to hers.

We heard him flush the toilet and come down the hallway. "Thanks for the cake, Val," he yelled, and closed his door. His bed must have been against the wall, because I heard him open a drawer, then sit down with a thump.

It was quiet for maybe two minutes. Next he said in a low voice, "What?" adding in a louder voice, "what! What? AAAHHH! Out! Out! EEEEEE!"

CHAPTER THREE

"What on earth?" My aunt came running upstairs, followed by my mother.

Valerie and I were already standing in the doorway to Jason's bedroom.

Jason was in his pajamas, sitting on his bed but with his back against the wall. He had stopped yelling and had his arms folded across his chest. "Very funny." He glared at his sister and me.

My aunt shoved between us and looked in. "Now what?" she said in an exasperated voice. "Oh, Jason. Really."

His sheets were pushed right back, and there, fat and green on the bed where his feet would have been, were the three frogs Valerie and I had found at the pond. They looked uncomfortable and their chins kept puffing out as if they were going to say something. Probably "Lemmee outta here! Now!"

The biggest frog went *brrack!* and

jumped from the bed and landed on the floor. Another jump and he was under the dresser.

"Jason, how many times have I told you? No animals in the house!"

It was amazing. My aunt was chewing him out, but she was still grinning. Shaking her head but smiling, as if to say, "What a kid!"

"Now, would you please gather these — these creatures up and take them outside! What must our guests think?" She folded her arms and shook her head once more.

Jason curled his lip and shot Valerie and me a dirty look. But he didn't say anything. Not a word. I had to hand it to him. He could have told on us, but instead he kept his mouth shut. I almost felt like getting down on my hands and knees to help get the big green guy out from under the dresser. Almost, but not quite.

Jason gathered up the frogs in an old shoe box from his closet and took them outside. Mom and my aunt hung around in the hallway for a while, talking about the goofy things kids do.

Then my mom yawned and said, "Well, I should go to bed, too, since I want to leave fairly early tomorrow morning."

Normally I give her a little hug before bed. But not this time. I just said, " 'Night," and went into my cousin's room. I wanted her to know what I thought of being dropped off like some little kid who had no opinions of her own.

"I want to get it painted pink," Valerie said a few minutes later.

We were lying under the sheets, and a small lamp on her desk was on. Her bedroom walls, which were white, went up a bit, then sloped toward the center of the ceiling. It was nice, like being in a little church. Well, sort of.

"The whole room pink. With blue-and-pink curtains. What do you think?"

"Looks fine the way it is," I answered.

Actually, it looked more than fine. Valerie's bedroom was probably the tidiest I had ever seen. My own was always a mess. Even though I helped Mom with the cooking and washing, I just couldn't seem to keep my room neat. Clothes littered the floor, books were heaped at the foot of the bed, and I never could do my homework on my desk because there was so much stuff on it. I usually gave up trying to put away hair clips and pens and my diary and simply studied my math on the kitchen table.

"What's your house in Edmonton like?"

"It's a town house. Two bedrooms and bathrooms upstairs, a living room and kitchen below those, and finally a basement. We call the basement 'No man's land.' Mom says if anything goes down there, it gets sucked into eternity." After thinking a moment, I added, "Our place is probably too big for just the two of us."

Valerie rolled over onto her stomach and looked across the bed at me. "Does your — ".

She never finished the sentence, but I knew she was going to ask me about my dad. I didn't want to talk about him, though, so it was quiet in the room. At last I said, "I'm sort of tired. Do you mind if we turn out the light?"

Although I fell asleep pretty fast, I woke up at least twice during the night. In the darkness, I could feel the strangeness of the bedroom.

I thought about my father.

The three of us had moved out together from Toronto and had been living in Edmonton for less than a year, when he left and went back to Toronto. He phoned, but not often enough.

I tried to sleep. First on my left side, then on my back and next on my right side. I even tried on my stomach, which I hate. Can anybody really sleep with a pillow mushed up against her mouth?

Valerie's room, so neat and perfect, shone

in the bluish light from the moon. Her breathing was soft and regular: inhale, followed by a long *ahh*, inhale — *ahh*, inhale — You get the idea. It was driving me nuts.

I sat up and turned on a lamp that was on the dresser. The light didn't seem to bother Valerie. Inhale — *ahh*.

My book was on the floor by my sport bag. I picked it up and thumbed through it, though I wasn't really in the mood to read. The pages opened to one of the hard parts of the novel, where Merlyn changes Wart into an owl.

As an owl, Wart flies over the Earth and learns how life is always changing. I guess he gets wiser somehow — I don't know. Maybe that was *my* problem: I didn't understand why Mom and Dad had broken up in the first place. Or why they couldn't make up and get back together. Or why Dad didn't phone me more often.

"Maybe you're just too dumb to understand these things," I muttered. Maybe I needed a magician to turn me into an owl, a wise old owl. Ha! What a stupid idea. If I could be anything, I'd rather be the peregrine, strong and fearless, able to go anywhere it pleased. Then nobody could — Suddenly I stopped myself. Who was I kidding? Even the peregrine could get shot, and its young ones were being stolen away from their parents.

I remembered the falcon chicks I had seen at the AGT tower in Edmonton, and imagined a man taking them from their nest and shipping them to some desert in Arabia. I knew how they would feel, all alone and abandoned with strangers. Angrily I hoped that Mr. Tessier and the police would find whoever was stealing them.

My cheeks were wet. I got out of bed, not knowing what to do. Without thinking, I hurled the book across the room, where it hit the wall with a thud. Valerie let out a little sigh, rolled over, but didn't wake up. Sure, now was I going to trash her room, too? Dumb, dumb. I pulled a tissue from a box on the dresser and sat down. Let's face it, Valerie's room was too neat to be trashed.

Her window was beside the dresser. I could put some clothes on, go outside and walk. Far away, out beyond the barn, a dog barked. It was a lonely sound.

Halfway across the country, my dad was asleep, and he didn't even know how I felt. In another part of this house, my mom slept, knowing how I felt, but not caring. Right then I hated them both.

I went back to bed. After tossing and turning some more, I dozed off.

CHAPTER FOUR

When I awoke in the morning, Valerie was already gone. The bedroom curtain was closed, but sunshine still seeped in around the edges of the windowsill. Her bedside clock radio said 9:30. My head hurt a little and I felt kind of fuzzy all over from not sleeping well.

Talk about a neat and tidy kid. Her bed was made, with the covers all smoothed out, and her nightshirt lay folded in front of her pillow. Some things about her were going to be hard to take.

I could hear voices outside, so I got up slowly — my head was throbbing pretty good now — and walked over to the window. When I pulled the curtain I could see that Valerie and her dad stood down below on the dirt driveway. He had on a pair of jeans and a jean jacket, and a cap with an Esso insignia on it. The window was up, but I couldn't quite make out what they were saying.

Then he put his arm around her shoulder, gave her a hug and walked toward the barn. Valerie waved and called, "See you at lunch!" Soon an engine rumbled, and my uncle passed in front of the barn on a big green tractor.

I don't like crying, even when nobody is around to see me. Besides, I had let myself do a bit of that the night before. So when I felt my throat go funny and my eyes get wet, I said, "Knock it off," and made myself stop. I hadn't seen my dad in almost three months, but he would be coming out to Edmonton soon. He had promised, and he always kept his promises. Still, I'd felt sad inside when I saw Valerie's dad give her that hug.

I got dressed and sort of straightened the covers on my cot. Then I went downstairs to the kitchen. My mom and Aunt Mary sat at the table, having coffee. I noticed my mother's canvas gym bag by the back door.

"So, all this fresh air's too much for you!" My aunt flashed me one of her smiles.

"Kim is actually the early riser around our house," my mom said. "I usually need her to pull me out of bed after I've turned off the alarm."

She was trying to be nice to me, trying to make her leaving less noticeable. I wasn't going to let her off the hook so easily.

"Yeah," I said. "Guess you're going to

have to get one of the neighbors to give you a wake-up call while I'm gone." She didn't like that — I could see it in her eyes. But she didn't say anything else.

My aunt, who didn't have a clue what was going on, just asked me if I wanted something to eat.

"Not yet, maybe some o.j. first, thank you."

While she poured the orange juice into a glass, Mom stood. "Well, guess I should be off then. I want to get the tire fixed at a garage and do some grocery shopping today, too." She came over to me, put her arm around my shoulder and squeezed.

She seemed stiff, though, and I thought right away of how Valerie and her dad had looked a few minutes earlier.

"Have a good time. I'll miss you." She stepped back to look at me.

I shrugged. "Sure. See you in two weeks."

We went out to the car with her and waved as she drove away. When the car had disappeared and the dust from the road settled back down, the farm was very, very quiet. You could see for miles, I thought, across fields to small hills that looked blue in the distance. If I had to live in a place like this, I would go nuts in a week. Wait a minute, dummy, I thought. You *are* going to be here that long! I took a deep breath and sighed.

Valerie was standing beside me. "Hey," she said, "want to see our horses?"

"You have horses?" I replied like an idiot. What did I expect them to have on a farm, camels?

"Yeah, two. Come on."

"Wait a sec." I ran into the house for my camera. "Who knows," I said when I got back, "maybe we'll see a camel."

Valerie gave me a puzzled look, laughed and led the way toward the red barn. As we crossed the broad open area between the house and the barn, I heard something from behind the house and turned to look. Jason, wearing a hockey helmet, came into view, driving one of those miniature tractors, the kind used for doing gardens and stuff. He let out a whoop and made straight for us.

Valerie turned to face him, putting her hands on her hips. When he was still about twenty feet from us, he swerved and made a looping circle, with us in the middle.

"He's showing off," Valerie said with a frown. "For you."

He made a couple of more circles, then spun off into a field.

"Your parents let him drive that thing?" I asked. "Isn't it dangerous?"

"My dad put something on it — a governor? — so it can't go very fast. And Jason is *supposed* to be careful."

"What did you mean when you said he was showing off for me?"

"Oh," she said, laughing, "haven't you noticed? Last night at supper, the way he kept looking at you? And the way he follows us around? Maybe I shouldn't say this because he is my brothcr, but I think he has a crush on you."

"A crush! But that's ridiculous! He's so young. Besides, we're — we're cousins. That's sick!"

"Oh, I don't think he wants to marry you or anything," Valerie said. "He just likes you, that's all."

I knew she was right, and that made it worse. I recognized the way Jason looked at me. Adam Spence in my class looked at me like that sometimes, too, although I didn't mind when he did it because he was cute. But your own cousin? Maybe it wasn't sick, but it definitely seemed a little weird.

Valerie flipped a wooden latch on a side door to the building and we went inside. It was cool and dark in the barn, and smelled of straw and animals. We walked through the barn to the back, where a big sliding door stood open. Outside again, I saw two horses, a black one and a cream-colored one. They were saddled and tied to a fence rail by their reins.

"I hope you don't mind. I got them ready

in case you wanted to go for a ride. Uh, you know how, don't you?"

"Know how what? Oh, you mean ride? Oh, sure. My dad and I used to go riding a lot together." Actually, we had gone once when I was about six years old. It was at a campgrounds, and the owner had taken us out for a half hour. The truth was, I realized, horses kind of scared me. I mean, they're so darn big. What if they just decided to take off? Nobody my size could stop one, that was for sure.

"Great! Come on." Val began untying the reins of the black horse, then stopped.

"What's the matter?"

"Well, this is Jason's horse, Blackie. So I guess we should ask him first if it's all right."

"Hey, if it's going to be a problem, we don't have to — " I began, but was interrupted by a voice from inside the barn.

"I don't mind. Go ahead."

Jason stood in the doorway of the barn, half in shadow. He had his hands in his pockets, as if he couldn't care one way or the other, but he was wearing this silly grin. Did he want me to get on, get thrown to the ground, so he could giggle his rear end off? I was trapped: if I admitted I knew a lot less about riding a horse than riding a skateboard, I would look like a fool.

"Thanks." My voice came out a little

strangled. I slung my camera over my shoulder and took the reins from Valerie's outstretched hand. The horse, Blackie, craned its neck to look at me. A huge dark brown eye rolled around as if to say, "Are you serious — you want to get way up *there* on me?" A fly buzzed around my head, made a pass at Blackie's face, and the horse's whole body shuddered. God, he was big.

"Easy." I patted his shoulder. It always helps to show an animal that you're calm. Who told me that? Oh, yeah, Mr. Smith, my paper-route manager. He said that if a dog attacked you, just act calm, because if you show that you're afraid, you'll upset the dog. Sure, but what if you *are* terrified?

Holding the reins, I reached up with my left hand, grabbed the saddle horn — thinking, hey, I even remember the names of these things — put my right foot in the stirrup and stepped up. Everything seemed so smooth.

I was up in the air, swinging my left leg up, when I realized what was wrong. If I went through with this mount, I would be on the horse all right, but facing backward! I stopped, awkwardly exchanging feet in the stirrup and flopping into the saddle.

Valerie was staring at me, her eyebrows arched.

For a second nobody said anything, then

Jason spoke. "Are you sure you know what you're doing?"

"Of course — " I began, and wanted to call him an idiot, but I stopped myself. If I kept pretending, I would only dig myself into a hole. "It's been a while," I said simply. "I've forgotten some things, I guess."

Valerie showed me how to use the reins to make the horse turn, go faster, slower and — most important to me — how to make him stop. We spent about fifteen minutes circling the fenced pasture. I began to feel good about riding, until she said it was time for the ride.

"We'll go toward the river. There's a place where we swim sometimes if the water's high enough, and . . . something else you might be interested in."

She exchanged a look with Jason. They seemed excited, and I sensed they were trying to make me happy. I liked them for that.

Valerie grinned eagerly. "Are you ready?"

"Uh . . . yeah." Riding around in a fenced-in area is one thing. The open prairie is another. But what did I have to worry about? Blackie answered my every command. Left, Blackie — no problem. A gentle pressure on his neck with the reins and amazing! We would go left.

"Great!" I said. "Let's go."

CHAPTER FIVE

Jason wanted to come along, and that was okay with me. He could handle Blackie if anything unusual happened. Besides, after the frogs-in-the-bed trick, he seemed to be trying harder to be an ordinary kid. Except for the fact that he still stared at me a lot. Funny, though. Even that didn't bother me much. It was sort of like having a fan.

Jason opened a gate, let us through, then closed it again. He got on behind Valerie and we headed out around a group of cattle and past the pond where the frogs for Jason's bed lived. Jason glanced once at the pond, said *ribbit*, and we laughed.

Everything was fine for about ten minutes. Once the barn was behind us, the land didn't look quite so flat. In fact, we were steadily going upward, through a series of small hills. Whenever we reached a rise, you could see for miles. The sun was getting hot, and the sky was so blue it made your eyes water. Two perfectly white clouds hung off to our right like giant scoops of ice cream. I began to think it was beautiful.

I hadn't noticed, but Valerie's horse, a mare called Madonna, I guess because of her cream color, had gotten steadily ahead. At first it had been only a length or two, but now it was about fifty feet. A couple of times Valerie had slowed down for me, but now she and Jason were talking, and I guess they didn't notice. I didn't, either. I was daydreaming.

Suddenly Blackie turned his head, his whole body, made a complete circle and started to go back.

"Hey, wait a minute. What are you doing?" I said in a low voice.

I pulled back on the reins. Nothing. Not even a pause. I tugged them to the left. He didn't even twitch. I pulled to the right. He shook his head, making his mane fly. Almost as if he were saying, "Uh-uh, no way, kid."

Blackie marched along back the way we had come. I looked back at my cousins. They hadn't realized what was happening.

"Blackie!" I jerked up on the reins. Valerie had said just to let the horse know who's the boss. Blackie stopped dead in his tracks. He turned his head and looked at me as if to say, "Well?" Then he took off again, this time faster.

"No. Hey. Stop. Whoa. Come on, knock it off!"

Blackie began to trot.

Time to bail out. I turned to yell, "Hey, gimme a hand here!"

Valerie stopped and wheeled her horse around. They came at a slow gallop, with Jason wrapped around her middle, bouncing up and down. She pulled across our path and stopped. Jason reached out and grabbed my horse's reins.

"Blackie! Behave!" He shook his finger at the animal, who actually hung his head.

"Sorry," Jason apologized to me. "He sometimes tries this with me. He just wants to go back and eat. He's always hungry. Look at the size of that belly. You have to lose some weight, boy." He reached out with his runner and gently tapped the animal's underside, which *was* considerably wider than Madonna's.

"We don't exercise them enough," added Valerie.

"Sometimes," Jason said, making himself look serious, "you have to use a little psychiatry on him." He reached into his shirt pocket.

"That's *psychology*, dummy." Valerie rolled her eyes.

Jason extended his hand and I saw he held a sugar cube. Blackie perked his head up and wrapped his lips over the cube. Immediately he began to turn and follow Madonna again.

"I know that psychology," I said. "My mom uses it on me all the time — 'Kim, if you want to go to that movie, you have to clean your room first.' "

"Yeah," Valerie said, nodding, "our dad does the same, only it's usually 'Okay, whose turn is it to shovel out the horses' stalls?' Believe me, cleaning a room is no big deal compared to shoveling out horse buns."

She had a point there. Maybe that was why her room was always so clean. We were riding more or less side by side now.

Jason glanced across at me. "Why did Uncle Murray move back to Toronto and not take you with him?"

Valerie drove an elbow into his chest. "Shut up!"

Jason turned white and gasped for breath. "Ow . . . ya didn't have to —" he gasped again "— I was just curious!"

We rode for a while in silence before I answered. "He and Mom weren't getting along. They're going to get a divorce pretty soon."

"Oh." Jason's voice was small.

Valerie spoke. "I guess you miss him a lot."

I thought of how she and my uncle had

looked that morning, and I felt my eyes get watery again. I glanced away a second. "Yeah, sometimes more than others. But," I added quickly, "he's going to be in Edmonton soon. For three weeks. So it's not so bad, really."

"Sure," Valerie was quick to agree, giving her brother a sidelong look. "And I'll bet you will get to visit him in Toronto, too. That would be neat."

"Uh-huh." I nodded. Dad had never asked me to come out for a visit. I wondered about that sometimes.

We walked the horses for almost a half an hour. Suddenly the ground sloped downward, and we were at the edge of a riverbank. The drop-off wasn't steep, but you couldn't see the edge until you were almost on top of it.

The horses stopped. Jason took off his glasses and wiped them with the front of his T-shirt. When he put them back on, he cleared his throat importantly and said, "We have something to show you, Kim."

Valerie smiled, rolling her eyes at Jason's grown-up act.

"Right over there — " he pointed " — is a falcon's nest. The bird is probably the same one you saw yesterday, the peregrine. The markings, how it flies — everything sounds the same."

"But," interrupted Valerie, "we never knew it was so special until you talked about it. This is exciting!"

So that was what they had been exchanging looks about at supper the evening before. This was great. In Edmonton we only got to view the nest on a television. I was probably the only kid in my class to see one close up and in person, twice even.

"Here's where we go down." Valerie pointed to a grassy depression.

"Before we do, can I just take one picture?" Below, I could see the river moving slowly, reflecting light. It all looked good, and I thought it would make a neat shot for my album.

I turned so that I could get a view of the river upstream with a bridge in the background. "Is that bridge for cars or trains?" I asked.

My cousins looked at each other and laughed. Valerie shrugged. "I think it's still for cars. At least, it was when you crossed it yesterday. Don't you recognize it? That's the same road you and your mom used to get to our place."

I craned my neck, pretending to look at the position of the sun and our location. "Oh. Oh, right. Sure, I was just a little mixed up there for a minute." One thing was certain: I'd better not try to find my way around out here alone. I'd get lost forever.

After I had the shot, I noticed something and I pointed. "There's a truck over there. See? Between the bushes." A green pickup was parked on the same side of the ravine as us, but far enough away to be hard to see.

"I don't recognize it," Jason said.

"Me, neither," added Valerie.

"It might be the patrolman who talked to us yesterday," I suggested. "His truck was the same color, but it's hard to tell from here."

"Well, let's get moving," Jason said impatiently, forgetting the truck.

Horses must be able to smell water, because they both seemed eager to get moving. Now, without even being directed, they started down the shallow ravine.

"The nest is just around the bend." Valerie pointed in the direction opposite the bridge, as our horses drank at the water's edge. There was a small sandy shore there, and the flat beach curved with the river.

"What's that?" Jason had slid off Madonna's back to wash his hands and face in the water. He was bending over now, peering at something we couldn't see.

Valerie got down, too. "A tent. Probably belongs to whoever owns the truck."

"Yeah? Let's go see." Jason was already walking in that direction.

Valerie pulled Madonna along and I gave Blackie a nudge with my runner.

The tent was pitched a little farther along than the truck, which disappeared from view above us as we got closer. It was green nylon, the kind that has poles at either end and can sleep two or three people. Jason circled to the opening of the tent and peeked inside.

"Jason!" called Valerie. "Don't be a snoop. What if somebody sees you?"

"Don't be a granny. I won't hurt anything." He stuck his head in for a moment, before standing up again. "Guess they must be fishing," he said. "There's a rod and a tackle box, with eggs and flies and stuff. But — " Then he stopped, as if he were trying to figure something out.

"What do you kids want?"

The voice came from behind us and startled me so that I nearly fell off Blackie.

CHAPTER SIX

A man emerged from the bushes, holding a pair of binoculars. He marched over to where Jason stood. Jason backed up and walked quickly over to stand beside his sister. "Nu-nuthin'," he stammered.

The man looked old — older than my dad, anyway — and he had a beard that matched his long gray hair. He glanced inside the tent, laid down the binoculars, then whipped the tent flap shut. When he came back to where we were, I could see that he was upset. His eyes had little crinkles in the corners, where they were squishing down hard and sharp.

"You figure if nobody was around, you were gonna maybe walk off with my brand-new equipment?"

"No way." Now Jason was getting mad.

If I hadn't been nervous about the man, I would have laughed. Jason was less than half the stranger's size, but he seemed ready to ask for an apology.

"We saw your truck up there —" Jason pointed above us "— and we were just curious to see who was here."

The man dropped a cigarette on the ground and mashed it under his boot. "I don't know what truck you're talking about," he said. "That's my car," he added, pointing to a brown station wagon partially hidden under some trees nearby.

The man crossed his arms before he spoke again. "I'm trying to have a little peace and quiet. Just want to get away from the city for a while and do some fishing." He shrugged. "I don't seem to be having any luck in this spot. Maybe move on in a while. Don't imagine a kid like you would know of any good places, eh?"

"My dad comes here once in a while. He says it's pretty good." Jason shrugged. "Maybe you're using the wrong bait."

"Yeah, you think so, young Mr. Expert?" The man frowned.

Nobody spoke, and the old guy glared at us.

Valerie pulled Madonna's head around. "We should get going," she said. She led the way, and Jason and I followed.

The man called after us, "Try not to make

so much noise around here. You're probably scaring the fish away."

We walked the horses along the river's edge, past the tent and under the bridge. Beneath the bridge it was cool and shadowy. A car hummed across overhead, then was gone.

Speaking with her head down, and not looking back, Valerie said, "He's not very friendly, is he?"

"And not too hot as a fisherman, either," Jason added.

"What do you mean?" I didn't want to ride while my cousins walked, so I stopped Blackie and stepped down as I asked the question.

"Well, the fishing rod didn't have line strung and none of the jars with bait in them had been opened. But there was something else, too, something kind of weird."

"What?" Val and I spoke at once.

"A cage."

"What kind of a cage?"

"Well, not big. About like this." He drew a shape in the air with his hands, roughly the size of a portable television. "It had bars on it, and a door in the front. Oh, and a handle on top."

Val frowned. "Was anything inside?"

"Nope. Empty."

"You know . . ." I began.

"Yeah?" They looked at me, waiting.

"Well, it's probably nothing, but I was wondering, how far is it to the nest?"

"Just around the bend, maybe three or four hundred meters beyond the bridge. Why?"

"Well, he was really unfriendly, like maybe he had something to hide. And it doesn't look as if he's really doing any fishing."

"So?"

"So yesterday the patrolman from Fish and Wildlife was very anxious, as if he expected someone to try to steal the young falcons in this area." I reminded them about the smuggling and export business in stolen falcons.

"He *is* camped awfully close to their nest," said Valerie.

"And there's the cage I saw," added Jason.

We stopped walking and looked back in the direction of the tent. I picked up a small stone and threw it into the water. "It's probably nothing. He's probably just a grouch who can't stand people."

"Right." Val chose a pebble and tossed it into almost the same spot as mine.

Jason put his hands on his hips stubbornly. "I still think he's an old poop." As if settling the matter, he added, "There sure was a lot of beer in the back of the tent, too. And that guy had already had a few. I could smell it."

"Mom says that's the real reason men go hunting and fishing — so they can lie around, drink and tell stories to one another." That popped out before I knew it. I could feel my cheeks getting red, as if I had let out some kind of family secret. My cousins couldn't have known, of course, but Mom said that after my dad had brought home one dinky little fish one weekend and about fifty empty beer cans.

Jason looked doubtful. "Yeah?" I could tell he didn't know about such things. Uncle John didn't strike me as the kind who sat around with a beer can and told dirty jokes to his friends. Funny thing, though, knowing that just made me miss my dad more.

We followed the river around the bend. The sandy shore narrowed, but the river was wider here. On the opposite shore, the bank rose steeply to cliffs a hundred feet or higher.

"Here," Jason announced.

Valerie nodded and pointed. "See there," she said to me, "up where the cliff seems to split? Where there's a flat spot about halfway up?"

As I looked to where she pointed, something moved in the spot.

"There she is!" Jason thumped my shoulder. "The mother falcon!" A dark brown head showed, then speckled shoulders.

I rubbed my arm. For a little guy, Jason had a hard fist.

"Can we get closer?" I asked.

"The river is shallow here, but we should leave the horses on this side. The bottom is kind of rocky," Valerie said. She chose a dead tree and we tied Blackie's and Madonna's reins together under the trunk.

The river flowed slowly, and the water was almost warm. The rocks on the bottom were smooth, so we had to be careful not to slip. But Jason did, and sat down with a splash.

"Quiet," Valerie told him when he let out a yelp. "We don't want to scare the birds."

Jason got up, looked at his bum, made a face but kept still.

When we finished crossing, Jason stood at the base of the cliff, looking up. "We can't see much here," he said. "We'll have to climb up for a better view."

"You *are* nuts!" Valerie was shaking her head.

Silently I had to agree with her. I like climbing trees, but this looked like the side of a mountain. Jason was already finding a hand hold and placing his runners along the ridge. Soon he was about ten feet above our heads.

"Good grief," Valerie muttered. "I'd better go along to see that he doesn't fall."

Jason turned to me. “Hey, Kim, this is a chance to get some great pictures!”

“Yeah, sure.” My voice quavered.

Of course, I wasn’t about to be left on the ground. And I *did* want a closer look at the falcons. I stopped to take my camera from my shoulder and snap a quick picture before starting to climb. I followed as they led the way along the steplike ridge that went up alongside the notch where the birds were. It was narrow and dirty. I tried not to look down.

“Hey, Kim, what did the man say on the way down when he fell out of the ten-story window?”

“Shut up, Jason.”

Valerie was puffing, and I noticed she didn’t bother to punch him.

“So far, so good. Ha-ha-ha.”

“That’s an old one,” I breathed. I didn’t look down.

At last we got to a point right opposite and about fifty feet away from where the bird had appeared. She was still there, and now she stared directly at us.

“There’s no nest,” Jason said. “She’s sitting on bare rock.”

“Peregrines don’t build nests out of twigs and grass like some other birds,” I replied.

Jason had taken off his glasses and, while leaning with his forehead against the cliff face, cleaned them on the front of his shirt. "Maybe they're tougher."

Or, I was tempted to say, dumber. As much as I loved these falcons, at that moment I wasn't feeling generous. Sitting on bare rock all day wasn't my idea of a lot of fun. Just then another head popped up behind the falcon. She shifted, and then we could see two more.

"They've hatched!" cried Jason.

"More than hatched. They look almost ready to fly."

The young ones had fatter-looking heads, and their feathers were fluffy, as though they had just come out of the clothes dryer. Suddenly the mother let out a scream and flew out from the nest. Circling over the river, she swooped by the cliff above us.

"I don't think she appreciates our being here," said Valerie.

At the same moment, Jason's eyes widened and he pointed with his free hand at the sky behind me. A sound, something like *hek-hek-hek*, came from above. I turned — and froze. A second falcon, the male, was flying into the gorge fast. He dove directly for us, as if going to attack. I cringed and scrunched my face into the rock.

There was a flapping sound, and I peeked out. The falcon was hovering a few feet above us, his beating wings brushing against the rock face!

"Move it!" Jason yelled. He was coming back down, crowding against his sister.

"I'm trying!" Valerie shot back, and turned toward me.

I had already reversed my direction and was moving as fast as I could down the ridge. Rocks dislodged and clattered to the bottom of the ravine. I remembered how climbing down is always harder than climbing up.

I was about three-quarters of the way, when I glanced back. Valerie was only a few feet above me with Jason right at her elbow. The falcon wasn't giving up. He swooped again, and this time I saw one of his wings swat Jason's head. Jason reached up to protect himself — and lost his balance.

I opened my mouth in a silent yell as I watched him fall to an outcrop of dirt, which immediately broke under his weight. He bounced, tumbled outward and landed in a heap, before lying still on his back.

"Jason!" Valerie screamed. "Oh, no! Hurry, let's help him!"

We both jumped the last part, and I heard her yelp "Ow!" behind me. Hurrying to Jason's side, I saw that his mouth was open and he was gasping for air. His eyes were wide as they darted from Valerie to me.

"He's had the wind knocked from him," I said. "It happened to me once. It's scary."

Soon he was breathing in big gulps. "Ah — ah — ah — oh, oh . . ." His face was red and he started to moan. Nothing seemed to be broken, though, as he rolled onto his hands and knees.

Valerie looked ready to cry. She kept touching him on the head, the back, holding his hand. "Are you all right?" she kept asking over and over.

At last he nodded, and we helped him to his feet.

"Are you sure you're all right?" she repeated.

"Uh-huh, I think so."

"Your back? I mean, you landed right on your back."

"Yeah, it's okay. Where's the bird?"

The female was back in her nest. The male was high overhead, watching. He cruised in a line parallel to the river, then reversed and passed overhead again.

I handed Jason his glasses, which had fallen safely a few feet from where he landed.

"Thanks," he said, grinning. "Boy, did you see that? A regular 8.9 double-gainer from the high dive board!"

He sounded brave, but I noticed that his hand, when he took the glasses, was shaking.

"Jason," Valerie asked seriously, "are you sure you feel fine?"

"Yeah. Bum's a bit sore, that's all."

"Good." With that, she wound up with a roundhouse right and hammered him in the shoulder.

The punch was so hard he stumbled backward, arms spinning like a pinwheel, and landed for the second time in the river. He sat down, wearing a stunned expression.

Valerie rushed up to him. She was livid. "You little creep! You almost killed yourself! You almost got all of us killed! I should break your stupid neck!"

He started to edge away from her in the water, crawling backward like an upside-down crab. "Aw, come on, Val. It's okay. Everything turned out fine."

"Fine! Fine! We get attacked by birds, you fall from a cliff and — and —" She stopped. "And now you're filthy. You might as well wash off while you're in there. Mom's gonna murder you."

She stood over him, glaring, as he splashed himself and rinsed his glasses in the water. He didn't say another word, either.

CHAPTER SEVEN

We continued upstream a little farther, where the ravine broadened again. A path appeared, and we headed for it. Water dripped from Jason, and Valerie refused to let him on Madonna until he had dried a little. Valerie simmered, and Jason had enough sense to keep his distance from her. She limped a bit. Every once in a while she took a sharp breath, which told me she was in pain.

"Guess we should be getting back. It must be almost lunchtime," I said, more to fill the empty space than anything else.

"We'll be lucky to get bread and water when my mom sees *this* mess." She jerked a thumb at her brother, who walked behind, staring at the ground.

"You're always picking on me," he whined.

"Because you're always such a dope. You get us into trouble all the time."

"Not true," he sniveled.

"Come on, hurry up. And stop wimping."

Valerie tried marching up the slope, tugging at the reins, but her limp slowed her down. Blackie needed no persuading from me: he already had the barn and eats in mind and nudged me in the back for more speed. We made the top of the ridge in a few minutes and decided to take the road home, since it would be smoother going for Valerie. We turned the horses back toward the road, mounted, and soon had them walking side by side on the dirt shoulder.

What happened next was so fast I barely had time to realize what was going on.

There was the sound of a vehicle approaching behind us, and Jason glanced around to see what it was. "Look out!" he yelled. At the same time he reined sharply, and the three of us jostled into the shallow ditch.

No sooner had we moved than a pickup truck shot past, straddling the edge of the road where we had been a second earlier. Dust and gravel flew. The horses snorted and wheeled, and I was afraid mine would take off across the fields. I grabbed him around the neck and said urgently, "No, no, that's all right. Fine, we're fine." Out of the corner of my eye, I noticed that the truck was skidding to a halt a short distance away.

The truck stopped — it was green, like the one we saw on top of the riverbank — and the driver's door opened. The driver leaped out and ran toward us, while the other man stayed in the truck.

"You kids okay?" He was a tall man, wearing dark green pants and a shirt with a crest on the pocket.

Though the horses were still skittish, we got them calmed down. Val glanced at me and her brother. "Uh, yeah. Guess so."

"Hey, I'm awfully sorry. I must have taken my eyes off the road for just a moment. Next thing I knew, we drifted right into the ditch and straight at you."

"You should pay more attention." The words were out of my mouth before I knew it. I was shaking, scared by the near miss.

"Yeah, you oughta be more careful," added Jason as he adjusted his glasses, which had slid down his nose.

For only a second, the man seemed ready to say something tough. His lips were pressed together in a thin line and he was squinting. Then his face relaxed.

"You're absolutely right. It was my fault. Mine entirely," he apologized. "Hey —" his face brightened "this is the second close call for you kids in less than an hour. That was quite the show back there by the river. You —" he nodded to Jason "— took quite a nasty fall. How are you feeling?"

Shrugging, Jason answered, "Oh, I'm fine. Just had the wind — How did you know that?"

"We're surveying along the ridge," the man said. "We saw everything from up here. At least, I did — through my spotting scope. We were going to rush down to help, but then I saw you get up. You seemed to have survived the fall."

"He'll live — until he gets home, anyway." Valerie tried to make her voice sound stern, but I could tell her anger was wearing off already.

The man chuckled. "You are quite a mess, son. Your folks will likely have something to say about that. Do you kids live nearby?"

"Not far. We're the first house over there if you follow the road. You're actually on our land now." Jason stuck his chin out.

One of these days, I thought to myself, someone is going to plant a fist on that chin. Grown-ups don't like smart-mouthed kids. Jason had obviously missed one of the first lessons you learn in school: no talking back to adults. On the other hand, I realized, I liked it when he stood up to the guy like that.

The driver of the truck ignored Jason's pushiness. "Oh," he replied, "then you must be the Schultz kids. Our company has some wells dug on your land — in the southeast corner."

Valerie nodded slowly. "The pumps are working again. For a long time they weren't."

"That's correct. Now that the price of oil has gone up, we can pump again."

"You're with an oil company?" I asked the question because he didn't look like what I thought an oil worker should look like: a muscular man who wore a hard hat and probably a jean jacket and boots. This man was slender, and though he did have on work clothes, they were really clean. And he wore runners.

"I should introduce myself," he said, holding out his hand. "Nick Bosley, and that's my partner back there." The man in the truck stayed where he was, still staring ahead, the back of his head to us. I could see part of his face in the side-view mirror of the truck, but he wore dark glasses. There was something familiar about him, but I couldn't think what, since the driver was talking again.

"Actually," the man next to me continued, "we have our own company. We do surveys and check for leaks in pipelines for the bigger companies."

He saw me reading the crest on his shirt.

"That's us." He tapped the blue patch, which said in black letters Protec Industries.

"Oh." I knew nothing at all about oil drilling, and began to feel uncomfortable as he stared at *my* chest.

"So," he said, "get lots of pictures?"

Right, not my chest, but my camera, which I had slung crossways over me. "Yeah, some."

"Nice camera. Bet it takes clear, sharp shots. My partner saw you aiming across the ridge, like maybe you might even have gotten us in one of the pictures."

"I dunno. Could be. I can't really remember."

My stomach was rumbling, and I was getting tired of talking with him. Even though he had apologized, I didn't like him because he struck me as kind of nosy. I gave my cousins a look. "We should get going. Valerie's ankle should be checked."

"Sure, I understand. Maybe we'll talk again some other time. You take care of that ankle, young lady. A sprain should be treated seriously."

He said goodbye with a big grin and walked quickly to his truck. He started up the engine, and with a cloud of dust the green pickup sped off ahead of us. During all that time, the passenger had not looked back once.

We set out slowly, with Valerie and Jason riding. I walked along in between the two horses.

"Do you get a lot of oil people coming out here?" I asked.

"Sometimes. Not often." Valerie bent over to rub her ankle. Already a puffiness around the ankle bone had appeared.

"How badly does it hurt?" I asked.

"I think it's swelling up."

It was getting red, too. I was glad we would be back before long. "I think we should take the rest of the day off. Boy, maniac drivers and mad hawks — glad I came to a boring place for some relaxation."

"And don't forget the old grouch," added Jason.

"Right. You know, the more I think about it, the more I doubt he was actually there to do some fishing."

"Maybe it's like he said — he just wanted to be alone. I mean, who would want to be around the sour old grump?" Jason turned up his nose, as if he had just opened the refrigerator and caught a whiff of a month-old leftover fish.

Ugh. I hate fish in the first place. My

stomach wanted food, and here my imagination was giving it pictures of rotten meat. Once I start thinking about something gross, though, I can't make myself stop.

"Have you guys ever seen what happens to oatmeal when you leave it too long in a container?" I asked. Dumb question. Their house was so clean, I doubted what I was going to say next had ever happened to them.

"No."

"These little mealy bugs hatch in it and start growing. They look like fat white worms."

"I used to like oatmeal for breakfast." Valerie's mouth pulled down at the corners, but she giggled.

It was Gross-out Time, and we knew it.

Jason was next. "Kim, have you ever seen a cow get the bloats?"

"Not lately, but I have a feeling you can describe it for me."

"The cow starts to fill up like a balloon with air. If you don't do something, it rolls over on its back with its feet sticking up at the sky and dies a horrible death." He leaned back in the saddle, his feet stretched out, his arms open wide and his tongue flopping from his gaping mouth.

"Barf. Can't anything be done to help them?"

"An enema's the best. You take a hose, stick it —"

"*Puhleeze*!" Valerie jammed her fingers in her ears.

We rode in silence for a few minutes. Then I said, "I have one more."

Valerie sighed. "If you have to."

"We used to have a station wagon before this car. A Chevrolet, I think. But we had to sell it." I paused, waiting.

"Well?" Jason poked me with his foot.

"Cut it out. You'll get my blouse dirty." The blouse already looked as if it had been used to wash our kitchen floor.

"Well, so we had to sell it because it smelled so bad."

"Smelled?" Valerie raised her eyebrows. "Why?"

"We couldn't figure it out, either. The smell started in June, just before school ended. It got a lot worse when the weather turned warm, so we had to drive around with the windows down all the time. Dad thought maybe the car needed to be cleaned, so we scrubbed it all over, but the smell was still there."

"What was the smell like?" Jason was grinning, loving it.

"Dirty socks that haven't been washed in a year, a dead animal — you name it. Thick and heavy — you could get a whiff of it even before you got close to the car."

"How could you stand it?" Valerie reached down and rubbed her ankle gently.

"Finally we couldn't. Dad took the car down to a mechanic. They took both the front and back seats out, and there it was! A half-eaten torpedo sandwich. Mine. I remember losing it one night on the way home from ballet, but I thought I had dropped it getting into the car."

"What did it look like?" Jason rubbed his hands together gleefully.

"Putrid. It was covered in green slime and had these little bugs crawling all over it."

"Positively revolting." Valerie placed a hand over her forehead in mock horror.

"Yeah," I agreed. "Now let's hurry home and eat."

CHAPTER EIGHT

"Well, it's about time! Your father was starving, so we've started already. We were getting worried about you. Where have —" Aunt Mary was about to put a slice of ham into her mouth, when she stopped to stare at us coming through the back door. "Valerie, what happened to you?"

Valerie's ankle was worse. She limped as we walked through the kitchen.

"I, uh, I tripped getting down from Madonna," she said.

"Let me see that," my aunt said, stopping Valerie. She bent over and touched my cousin's left ankle.

"Ow!" Valerie winced.

"Just look at that, John. It's swollen."

"Umm." My uncle craned his neck to peer down beside the table. "Say you did that getting down from the horse?" His eyebrows arched and he smiled a little. He didn't seem to believe the story. "Should be more careful." He looked at Jason, then at me.

I nodded, but looked straight at the ankle and not at him.

"You're going to have to stay off that foot for a while," my aunt said. "We might even have to take you in to see Dr. Feschuck."

"Aw, Mom, it's okay, really."

"Don't argue. Now, everybody wash up and have something to eat. Jason —" my aunt seemed to have noticed him for the first time " — what on earth have you been up to? You're filthy!"

Jason laughed. "I fell in the river."

Aunt Mary held her head in her hands. "You kids. Honestly, you have to have a shower and — no, no, have lunch first so I can clear the table. As if there isn't enough laundry already and . . ."

Mothers are like that. They worry about things like dirty wash and stuff. My mom gets upset whenever, as she says, "things get out of hand." Then she looks sad and depressed and watches a lot of TV.

We went down the hallway to the bathroom, washed up and returned to the kitchen. There were lots of good things to eat, and I was famished. Homemade sausage, peas from the garden and for dessert, strawberries and cream.

"So, what did you do this morning?" My

uncle had finished, and he leaned back in his chair as he used a toothpick on one of his side teeth.

"Went horseback riding." Jason took another helping of sausage. For a little kid, he sure ate a lot.

"I figured out that much myself. Valerie said she hurt herself getting off the horse, remember?" My uncle smiled, as if he knew the whole story already.

"We went down to the river. Dad, did you know that the oil company had some people doing work by the ravine?"

Uncle John stood, stretched and walked over to a calendar on the wall beside the refrigerator. "Got a letter from them last month. Supposed to have a crew out later this month. They're a bit early. Did you see them?"

"Yeah. And some old grouch parked by the river near the bridge. He said he was fishing, but he didn't seem to be doing anything but drinking beer."

This news interested my uncle. He turned, his eyebrows arching again. "What did this man look like?"

Jason described the stranger's appearance. When he finished, my uncle said, "Maybe I should drive over and meet this fellow. Never can tell."

I thought of the falcons and what the

officer had said to Mom and me about people stealing the birds. Trying to keep the excitement in my voice steady, I asked, "What do you think he might be doing?"

"Oh, probably nothing. But we have to be careful. There has been some rustling in the area in the past year."

Rustling? I pictured an old cowboy movie I had seen once. Men in dark hats sneaked up during the night and drove some cattle away from a big cattle drive. Later a posse of deputies, all wearing white hats, caught up with the rustlers, and there was a shootout. I couldn't believe rustling still happened in modern times, and said so to my uncle.

"Oh, it happens all right. Last year we lost one steer, and Smithson down the road lost three head." My uncle frowned, as if deeply disappointed.

"Did you ever catch the thieves?" I asked. I had visions of my uncle riding his huge green tractor, chasing men in black hats down the road that went past the farm.

"The police did. As things turned out, it was some people not far from here. Neighbors."

He shook his head, making a sad face, as though he could not believe one of his own neighbors would do such a thing. Then he went out, saying he had to put new spark plugs in the tractor. Jason wiped his mouth and quickly followed him.

"Jason, you will still have to change —" my aunt began, but shrugged. "He'll only get the new clothes dirty again. You girls may as well wash up now."

Valerie didn't take long. She showered, changed into fresh clothes and lay down on her bed. Aunt Mary fussed over her. "Now stay here for a bit, rest that ankle. I'll check on you after I do some gardening. Kim, just make yourself at home. There are towels in the bathroom closet."

She went outside, and I undressed in the bathroom. I put my dirty things in the hamper and hung Valerie's bathrobe on a hook behind the door.

Dust was in my hair and down my neck, so I washed my hair in the shower first. When I was done, I put the drain stopper down and filled the tub for a bath. Mist filled the bathroom. I felt relaxed. In all, it had been a good day, and I was having more fun than I thought I would. I put my head back and closed my eyes.

I must have fallen asleep, because when I opened my eyes again the water felt much cooler. Someone was in the house. That someone was now coming up the stairs. Better get out and get dressed, I thought.

I stood just as Jason pushed open the

door and walked in. He had gotten as far as the toilet and raised the lid, when he turned his head and caught sight of me. His mouth dropped open in amazement and he stood still, bending over, his hand still on the toilet lid.

"What are you doing in here?" I demanded. I tried to cover myself with my hands, but didn't know what to cover and what to leave uncovered, so I sank back down into the water.

"I, uh, I didn't, ah, know — you know — that you were, ah . . ." His face was blank, but he didn't make a move to leave, either.

"Look," I said, "if you're not going to take a picture, then maybe you'd better get out."

"Oh, yeah, sure. Hey, I didn't mean, you know —"

He let the lid drop onto the toilet with a crash and turned quickly. Unfortunately, the bathroom door had swung halfway shut again. He took a half step — and walked into the door with a *thunk*.

"Ow! Oh, no. Ouch." He grabbed his nose — and knocked his glasses off.

When he made a grab for the glasses, I could see blood already running from his nostrils.

"My nose! My nose!" Tears of pain sprang from his eyes.

Afraid he might fall and hurt himself

more, I ordered him to sit down. “Over there on the toilet,” I said.

Pinching his nose with one hand, Jason backed up and sat down blindly. Good thing the seat was down, or he would have gone right into the bowl. I pulled the shower curtain before me and stretched out to pick up his glasses.

“Here.” I handed them to him. Next I reached around, spun off a wad of toilet paper and gave that to him. It was damp from my wet hand, but he didn’t seem to mind.

“Tilt your head back and pinch your nose with your fingers.”

“Oday. I get lods of nodesbleeds. Bud dis one hurd.”

“No kidding. You really whacked it.”

So there we were. Me in the tub, starting to shiver, and Jason on the toilet, holding a wad of white Charmin streaked with red. That’s when it occurred to me. Other than my dad, who didn’t really count, Jason was the only male who had ever seen me with my clothes off. Knowing that made me wonder.

“Jason.”

“Ungh.”

“Have you ever seen a naked girl before?”

“Whaddd?”

“You heard me. Have you?”

He kept his head aimed straight ahead, but his eyes rolled in my direction. I kept the shower curtain between us.

"Uh, no! Well, maybe Valerie once."

"Valerie. Oh."

"Yeah, but you're bigger." His eyes darted to the side again.

"No, I'm shorter than she is."

"I mean —" he took his hands away from his nose and patted his chest "— here."

Downstairs, the kitchen door opened and closed. Jason got up and hurried out of the bathroom. I yanked the plug and got out. After quickly pulling on Valerie's bathrobe, I slipped into her bedroom and closed the door. Valerie was sleeping, so I put on a fresh pair of blue cotton pants and a shirt. Watching myself in the mirror, I buttoned the shirt all the way right to the neck.

I studied myself. Front, then sideways for a profile. There was a little bulge at my chest. Well, okay, maybe bigger than little. Obviously big enough to notice. Mental note: talk to Mom about getting a bra.

I went to the closet and put on my nylon windbreaker. Clouds were forming and it might rain later in the afternoon or evening.

As I walked down the hallway, I saw Jason sitting on his bed. He was gently rubbing his nose.

"Stopped?" I asked.

"Yeah." He looked at me sheepishly. "I'm sorry. I didn't mean to peek at you in there."

I shrugged. "It's partly my fault. I should have shut the door. Mom and I never do at home, so I forgot."

I left him there and went downstairs. My aunt had cut some rhubarb and was cleaning it in the sink. She said hello to me and asked, "Where are your cousins?"

"Valerie's fallen asleep, and Jason is lying down in his room. He has a nosebleed."

"A nosebleed. Good heavens, those two are in terrible shape today. You poor thing, you're going to have to make do and talk to me. Hope you aren't bored."

"No. Believe me, Aunt Mary, I'm finding the farm a lot more interesting than I thought it would be."

CHAPTER NINE

When Valerie woke up, her ankle was swollen worse than ever. She made it down the stairs to the kitchen, but she couldn't put much weight on her left foot.

"That settles it," Aunt Mary said. "We're going to have Dr. Feschuck look at your ankle."

Uncle John had taken the tractor out into the fields, so my aunt used a CB in the front porch to tell him we were going into Drumheller. Then we left the house, taking one of the cars. There seemed to be quite a few cars and trucks on a farm.

"A lot of them don't run," Jason said when I asked.

"Yes, but your father simply can't bear to part with them," my aunt added from the front seat. "Mind you, I suppose I'm just as bad. See that blue coupe over there?" She pointed to a two-door car that seemed to float in weeds beside a shed. "John proposed marriage to me in that old Ford. Somehow it wouldn't be right to take it to the dump."

Drumheller is about thirty minutes away from the farm, so I guess they aren't so isolated, after all. We coasted down a long, winding road as we approached town. Cliffs on either side of us were streaked with different colors, and some cliffs had little caps on top.

"Pretty steep ravine," I remarked.

"Coulee," Valerie corrected me. "We call them coulees."

"Oh."

"I like going into the Drum." Jason had turned around in the front seat to face us.

"Yeah?" I looked at the signs that came into view as we got into town, including one with a huge green, toothy dinosaur painted on it. "What's here?"

"Stuff."

"And I want you, mister, to stay out of the video arcade." My aunt shook a finger at Jason, and he made a face.

We turned off the main highway. I saw some stores, a pizza joint and a couple of motels. At one intersection, I could see the other end of "the Drum." Small is a good way to describe it. No McDonald's arches in sight. Still, I might find some interesting things here, too.

"Do we have to go in?" Jason asked as his mother pulled to a stop in front of a small white building with a sign that announced we were at the doctor's office.

"I suppose not," my aunt said. "But try to stay close by. I don't want to have to hunt for you later. We shouldn't be long." She held the office door open, and Valerie hobbled inside.

Jason and I headed down the street to where the stores were. He was quiet for a while before turning an anxious face to me.

"Kim," he blurted, "I want you to know I didn't walk in on you on purpose back there at the house. In the bathroom," he added unnecessarily.

I glanced at him suspiciously. If it had been anyone else, like Gary Tillis at school, I might have thought he was teasing, apologizing when he really had enjoyed seeing me standing there in my birthday suit. But this was Jason. He could tease and be a nuisance, but now his face wore an uncomfortable expression. In fact, his face was red, and I realized he was blushing.

"Forget it," I said. "I mean, nothing happened, right?"

"Right." A pause. "Thanks."

"No prob. So, where are we going?"

"Umm, we could go to the bowling alley. They have video games and pinball there."

"What about your mom?"

"Who's going to tell her?"

"Right."

We started along the sidewalk. I was feeling kind of lazy and relaxed, just looking up and down the street and soaking up the sun. Across the road was a newer building with a flagpole in front, some kind of government place. I noticed a green-and-white pickup with a rack of lights on top parked in front, at about the same time the front door to the building opened and Mr. Tessier, the nice officer my mom and I had met, walked out.

"Hey —" I grabbed Jason by the sleeve " — let's cross here."

We cut across the street on an angle that took us right past the truck.

As the officer placed his hand on the door handle, he saw me and smiled. "Hello, again."

"Hi." I stopped and put my hands in the back pockets of my pants. I was giving him one of my bigger grins, hoping I looked comfortable and casual. Mom was right. He was kinda cute — for an older guy. "Is this where you work?"

"The office is in there." He jerked a thumb over his shoulder. "But I try to stay away as much as possible. It's more fun in the field."

"Yeah, right." All of a sudden, I realized we didn't have much to say, and it felt kind of awkward. "Umm, how are the falcons doing?"

He looked at me with the same brief flash of suspicion he had the other time, but it faded quickly. Then he tapped his forehead. "Oh, yeah, you're *not* the smuggler. I remember now."

I liked that. He had a sense of humor, too.

"Funny you should ask, though," he continued. "We found a nest that had been knocked to the ground about fifteen minutes' drive north of here. Eggs were busted, and the parent birds had disappeared. From the looks of it, some amateurs were trying to get a souvenir. Too sloppy for the pros."

North was the opposite direction from my cousins' farm. If the conservation officers were busy at the damaged nest, I thought, they might not know that there was someone close by the "secret" nest Valerie and Jason had shown me.

"There's some —" I began, but Jason had turned his back to the officer and faced me now, his lips shaped in a silent "No."

"Some what?" Mr. Tessier asked.

"Uh, some pretty crummy people around, if they would destroy nests and stuff just to have a souvenir or something."

"You can say that again." He turned as if to leave. "How are you and your mother enjoying your stay?" he asked. Then he looked past me, taking in both directions of the street.

I thought I noticed disappointment in those blue eyes when they didn't see what they'd expected.

"Pretty good. My mom had to go back to Edmonton, though."

"Left you on your own, eh? Well, I'm sure you can handle it." He seemed ready to say something, but just shrugged instead. "I have to get going. See you around."

He got into the truck and drove north. I was getting pretty good at telling directions just by the position of the sun in the sky.

"Why didn't you let me tell him about the old guy by the river?" I asked Jason.

"Valerie and I — and now you — are the only ones who know about the nest. We don't have to tell the whole world."

"But it's his job to know. Besides, he probably already does."

Jason shrugged and started down the sidewalk. "Not necessarily. I haven't seen him before. Anyway, my dad says there are already too many people traipsing across our fields. This guy would just make one more."

Jason was acting as if the nest and the birds were his own somehow, and in a peculiar way, I could understand how he felt. If you let adults in on everything, pretty soon they're trying to run your whole life.

We passed a women's clothing store, then a bank, and a hotel with its side door open. Next to that was a Marshall Wells store. Suddenly Jason grabbed my sleeve. "Look, it's him!"

Coming out of the Marshall Wells was the man we had met by the bridge earlier in the day. He stopped in front of the store to put his wallet in his back pocket. As he did, he held something wrapped in a store bag under his arm.

"He bought some rope," I said, getting a clear glimpse of a coil sticking out of the bag.

"Yeah," Jason said. "Wonder what a stream fisherman needs rope for?"

Just then the man shifted his gaze toward us, and we quickly turned around to look again past the bank. After a moment we peeked back — to find him striding in the other direction.

"Let's see where he goes," I suggested.

"You mean, follow him?"

"Yeah. Or we could play video games if you'd rather." I grinned to show I knew which he would choose.

We set off about half a block behind the man, carefully keeping our distance. He walked quickly, swinging the bag. Reaching the end of the street, he halted for a moment, as if confused, then started off again to his left. When Jason and I reached the intersection, we saw him crossing the parking lot of a Co-Op. We watched as he entered the building.

"What should we do now — go in, too?" Jason asked.

"He might spot us. Let's try to get closer to the front window."

We skirted the parking lot and stayed close to the side of the building. It was shady there and the building felt cool as I leaned my bare arm against it. One step around the corner, and we had a clear view inside the store through the plate glass. The stranger was standing only about ten feet from us, his back turned as he talked to a clerk.

"What's he pointing to?" Jason demanded.

"It's —" I had to squint because light glinted off the glass " — some kind of bag with drawstrings." I couldn't see clearly, but the bag was rolled, green and appeared to be made of canvas or some other strong material.

"He could use the bag to hold fish or —" Jason began.

"Or young falcons," I finished for him. "And the rope would come in handy for climbing up that ravine."

We slipped around the edge of the building again. Jason's eyes behind his glasses were large. "We should tell somebody, don't you think?"

"Tell them what? That some grouchy old guy has been buying rope and bags? They would think we were silly. No, we have to know more exactly what he's planning to do."

Just then we heard the door to the store open and, in a moment, footsteps. The man passed by us only a few feet away, heading back to the center of town. When he was opposite a tiny hairdressing shop, he turned abruptly and disappeared from the sidewalk.

"Come on." I pulled Jason by his arm. "He's gone down an alley."

We charged across the street, our runners flapping on the hot pavement, and we covered the stretch of sidewalk in seconds. At the corner of the alley we lurched to a stop. I peered around the hairdresser's.

The alley went for about a hundred yards before coming to a tee at the back of a big old brick building. Except for a pile of junk, including an old bed, the alley was deserted.

“Where is he?” Jason whispered.

“Can’t see him. He’s already gone.”

We stepped cautiously into the alley. Weeds grew alongside the gravel road, and old newspapers and broken glass lay beside the building on our right. To our left, a high tumbledown fence hid some kind of lot. We passed a couple of closed doors and boarded-up windows. When we came to the end of the tee, we paused. The man was nowhere in sight.

“Great, now which way do you think he went?” Jason scuffed the dirt impatiently with his shoe.

“Right behind you, Mr. Buttinsky.”

Once my mom rented a couple of movies to watch on our VCR. She had never seen *Jaws*, she said, and she wanted to know if I’d like to. Some of my friends had seen it and said it was neat, so I thought, yeah, why not, you know? Well, you remember the first time the shark comes out of the water and the guy is sitting in the boat? I almost wet my pants. That’s how I felt when I heard the voice behind Jason and me.

I let out a squeak and whirled around. Jason jumped and dug his fingers into my arm.

“Wha-what do you want?” I managed to stammer.

"I think I'm the one who should be asking you the same — say, aren't you the girl I saw out at the bridge?" He turned to Jason. "And you, aren't you the snoopy little kid who was poking around my camp?"

When Jason didn't answer, he took a step closer. "Why are you two sneaking around, following me?"

"We're not following you," I lied. "We were just walking around, and we took a shortcut down the alley."

"Ha! I saw the two of you back there at the bank and then again outside the Co-Op. The clerk noticed you two hanging around outside and asked me if you were *my* kids. What a joke! As if I would have such unmannerly brats as you two."

"I'm no brat, you old —" Jason began.

But I grabbed the back of his shirt and gave it a tug to make him shut up.

It was too late. The man shifted his packages under one arm and reached forward to grab my cousin.

"I'm going to teach you a lesson, you bad-mouthed punk!"

Before the man could reach him, I spun Jason around and yelled, "Run! Now! Let's go!"

We tore off with the old man yelling and, I saw as I looked over my shoulder, trying to chase us. But he couldn't keep up. We made our escape down the left arm of the tee and came out on another street. Crossing that, we cut through another short alley, to find ourselves in front of a large building shaped like an upside-down cup.

"In there . . ." Jason panted. "Bowling . . . out of sight."

We hit the metal doors full tilt and ducked inside. Right away, I could hear the crash of pins being hit by bowling balls. A woman reading a magazine by the front desk looked up, so we slowed to a stroll.

Jason led the way over to a pinball machine, dug in his pocket for a quarter and pumped it in. I waited until he had the first ball bouncing off the flippers, then slipped over to the door to check outside. There was nobody in sight.

I returned to stand beside Jason. "Boy," I said, nudging him in the shoulder, "you should have seen yourself jump when he came up behind us."

"Hey, take off. You made me miss that shot." He frowned. "I wasn't scared. If he had tried to lay a hand on me — or you — I'd have let him have it." He held up a clenched hand.

"Sure." I shook my head. I couldn't get over how a kid as little as Jason was so spunky. It was funny, but probably dangerous, too. "You'd better watch who you take on, you know," I said. "You could get yourself creamed."

He jerked the plunger on the machine and sent another ball careering through the black mouth of a space alien. The steel bearing hit a bumper and rolled against a bonus pad, and Jason let out a whoop. He jerked the machine, triggering an alarm somewhere in its innards.

Bringg! Bringg! A red light flashed under the scoreboard: *Tilt! Tilt!*

"Sometimes," I observed, "a person can be too tough."

CHAPTER TEN

"Do you see him anywhere?"

I stepped cautiously from the doorway of the bowling alley and looked both ways down the road. No gray-bearded man in sight. "It's clear. Let's go," I said to Jason, who stood behind me.

We walked from the bowling alley to the doctor's office without wasting any time. I thought for sure that the old man would be looking for us, but he was nowhere to be seen.

Valerie and my aunt were coming out just as we opened the door. "Well, this is lucky," my aunt gushed. "We're finished and so are you. What did the two of you do? Hope you didn't get bored having to wait, Kim."

"Nope." I forced myself to keep a straight face, but when my aunt looked away, I made a sign to Valerie, tell you later!

Valerie had an elastic bandage around her ankle, and she walked stiffly. When we got into the car, she said, "I have to stay off it as much as possible for the next few days. Now *that's* boring!"

On the way back to the farm, we rolled up the car windows and my aunt turned on the air conditioning. Between the whooshing air conditioner and my aunt's constant chatter about the visit to the doctor's, nobody else in the car said much.

Valerie leaned over at one point to ask in my ear, "What've you two been up to?"

But at the same time my aunt shouted over her shoulder to the back seat, "Kim, didn't you have your appendix out last summer?"

We were turning off the main road by the time she stopped asking me questions.

"Now what!" My aunt slowed the car as we approached the house. A swirl of dust caught up to us, blanketing the car. In the yard was an RCMP cruiser, its special blue-and-white color combination hard to miss. Its flashers must have been in the grille, but the markings on the door were obvious.

"Oh, I hope nothing's happened to —" Aunt Mary began, before she saw my uncle and a policeman step from the house to the back porch. Forgetting us, she jerked her door open excitedly.

Jason and I helped Valerie get out. My uncle was explaining things to my aunt as we joined them, and he sounded puzzled.

"Just the back door forced. A few things tossed around in some of the rooms, but nothing missing as far as I can see. You should check though, Mary."

"But . . . but, why?" my aunt sputtered. "Who on earth — whatever could they — I mean, it seems so senseless to break in and not take anything. Whatever is this world —" She was talking to each one of us in turn, or I should say, *at* each one of us.

The policeman interrupted her. "Whoever it was may not have found anything he wanted. Money, drugs, whatever."

"Drugs! We certainly do not —"

"Mary, calm down. He's not suggesting anything."

My uncle put his arm around her and gave her a little squeeze. I used to think my mother got upset easily, but she loses the prize to her sister, that's for sure.

The policeman shrugged, then slipped a pencil into his shirt pocket. "Or maybe something scared them away. The dog, for example." He cocked his head in the direction of Ralph, who was milling around our legs, panting and every once in a while licking my hand.

My uncle began to laugh. "One thing this

hound is not is a watchdog. What exactly do you do around here, Ralph?"

Hearing his name, Ralph sat down and whined, before stretching out on the ground and rolling over on his back, his legs in the air.

"Actually, he's another member of the family. Goofy, like the rest of us," my uncle added. "I only came back from the fields because I saw dust rising from the driveway. I thought you'd finished early at the doctor's. When I drove up no one was here, but the back door had been broken open."

My uncle pulled the open door forward for us to see.

"Dad!" Jason leaped forward, snatching his father's hand away. "Don't touch anything — fingerprints, you know!"

My uncle looked sheepish. "Too late. I didn't think, and I'm afraid I waltzed in and handled a lot of stuff before I phoned the police."

Jason groaned. "Ah, Dad, don't you watch 'Murder She Wrote'?"

The Mountie held the screen door open. "Could I ask the other members of your family — not Ralph — to check for missing articles?"

We all filed in, then went through each room of the house. I followed the others, mostly listening as they tried to figure out what might be gone. I realized it wasn't easy trying to remember exactly what had been in a room.

My uncle supported Valerie up the stairs, and we all crowded into her bedroom. She opened her top drawer, where she kept her underwear. I noticed her cheeks get a little red as she hobbled to one side so that the policeman couldn't look in. Under a pile of panties was a wooden jewelry case, which she took out and opened.

She removed a small roll of bills, took off the rubber band around it and counted.

"Twelve, fourteen, fifteen. Nothing's missing here." After carefully rewrapping the money and replacing it in the jewelry case, she returned the case to the drawer and shut it.

"Do you notice anything else out of place, anything that looks as if it might have been moved?" The policeman was taking notes on a small pad, but he yawned once as he scanned the room.

I couldn't help thinking that his eyes, whether he knew it or not, were taking in a miracle. Now, if we had been in my room, the story would have been different: bed unmade, sheets trailing on the floor; drawers open, underwear spilling over as if trying to escape from prison; books stacked on the desk, the floor, the bed; notes to myself taped to the door.

It would have taken a month to figure out if anything was missing from my room.

Nope, I said to myself with a sigh, not one thing is out of place in this bedroom. Nothing would *dare* be out of place!

"Well, then, we have only the boy's room to check, so —"

"Wait!"

Shocked, everyone turned to stare at me.

I felt a chill along my neck as I raced first to Valerie's desk and tore open the drawers, then dropped to the floor to look under her bed.

"Kim, what is it? What's the matter?" My aunt placed a hand on my shoulder, but I ignored her as I flew to the closet. I looked inside, pushing aside clothes and checking the floor.

"My camera," I said from inside the closet. "I'm sure I left it on the bed or —" I paused, looking across the room " — on the desk. Do you remember seeing it, Valerie?"

She shook her head. "I thought it was in here, but . . ."

I looked questioningly at Jason.

His face was blank as he said, "I thought you hung the camera with your sweater, by the back door."

"It was there this morning, but I brought it upstairs after we came back from the river." Even so, I ran out of the room, down the stairs and through the kitchen. But the hook was bare. I went back upstairs more slowly.

They were silent, waiting, as I entered the room. The policeman's eyebrows were raised, and his pencil hovered above his notebook.

"Not there." I said. "I'm positive I left it on the bed."

I touched the coverlet to indicate the spot and sat down.

"Can you describe the camera for me, Miss —"

My aunt interrupted, "This is my niece, Kim Rysen. She's visiting us from Edmonton. Oh, Kim, I'm so sorry. And the camera was special, I know." She sat down beside me.

"It was a Ricoh." I spelled out the name. "Black, with a built-in flash. And a zoom lens." I had a perfect image of the camera in front of my eyes. I could remember exactly how it felt, how heavy it was. I remembered the first picture I took with it, of Mom with her arms around Ruffles.

"It was a present from my dad. I've only had it for —" I had to stop because my throat was suddenly thick and tears had welled in my eyes. I wiped a hand across my face and made myself not cry. Looking up at the policeman, I asked, "Why would somebody take my camera and nothing else, not even money?"

He poked the pencil in his hair and rubbed thoughtfully. "I honestly don't know, miss."

After the policeman left, the three of us kids sat in a lawn swing at the back of the house while my aunt made supper. Jason took the middle spot, using his foot to push the swing every once in a while.

I refused to talk about my camera, and for a few minutes we were all silent.

Then Valerie said, "Hey, now you can tell me what happened in town."

Jason and I took turns describing our run-in with the old man.

"What do you think the rope and canvas were for?" Valerie asked.

"You could use a rope for climbing," I said.

"And the canvas bag to put the birds in," added Jason.

Frowning, Valerie thought for a moment. "Maybe we should tell Mom and Dad. They could phone the police, or that Fish and Wildlife guy."

The swing carried us gently back and

forth as we each considered the possibilities. Jason stuck his foot out and gave us another shove every time the swing started its arc backward. When he got it going fast enough, the hinge made a squeak. *Swing. Squeak. Swing. Squeak.*

"Quit it, Jason. That noise drives me crazy." Valerie let her good foot rub against the ground to slow the swing down.

When it had returned to its former rhythm, Jason grinned slyly at me. He turned to Valerie, putting his face beside her ear. "Squeak, squeak, squeak."

Of course she elbowed him in the ribs.

"Seriously, what do you think we should do?" she asked me, while Jason groaned and held his side.

"I dunno. If we tell anybody else, what can they do? The old man hasn't actually done anything wrong yet, has he?"

"We don't know that. Maybe he's the one who stole the birds before. Don't forget, he had that cage."

We fell quiet again.

Inside the house the phone rang and my aunt appeared at the window. "Kim, it's for you."

"Me?"

"Yes. Your mother. Hurry, it's long distance, you know."

Only one day had passed since she'd

brought me to the farm. I hadn't really expected her to be phoning so soon. I wondered if something was wrong.

Maybe the sink was clogged again and she'd say, "Hurry, Kim. Catch a bus back to Edmonton. I need your help!" I'd answer, "Well, now, wait a minute, Mom. I mean it was *your* idea for me to come out here in the first place."

I could let her beg for a few minutes before agreeing to come back. Besides, life here was getting more interesting all the time.

I went inside, picked up the phone and sat down on a kitchen chair, draping my legs over it as if it were a horse. Vaguely I wondered if there would be time for another ride after supper.

"Hi, Mom."

"Hello, Kim. How are things working out? I hear you had some excitement there today."

"Yeah, somebody broke into the house. Took my camera."

"Aunt Mary told me. I'm very sorry, Kim. Maybe the police will find it right away."

I didn't answer. I felt like saying, "Yeah, sure. What do you care?" I remembered what she said when I'd first got the camera, that it was way too expensive for a young girl. "Your father's only trying to spoil you," she had added.

There was silence on the phone. Then I heard Mom clear her throat.

"Well, so otherwise, things are fine?"

"Okay, I guess. I went horseback riding this morning."

"You did? That's wonderful!"

And that's just like my mom. She wanted so much to think that she was right, that she had made the right decision.

That's why she and Dad had fought all the time: they were so much alike, both wanting to think they knew the best way in everything. Which is why I let her know about the horses immediately. But I didn't want to let her off easy.

"I got thrown from my horse, though," I said. And then, when I heard her horrified gasp at the end of the line, I added, "Just kidding, Mom. Don't faint."

"Don't do that, Kim. You know I worry about you."

We talked a little more, about the weather and the farm. She told me she would go to a movie that night. She didn't mention Al, but I knew that's who she'd go with. I could have made a remark, but I let it go.

"So —" her voice sounded funny " — your father hasn't phoned you today?"

"No. Why?"

"Well . . . he called here about an hour ago. That's why I called. I thought he would have talked to you by now."

Something peculiar was going on. Then I realized that she had phoned because she thought she should after speaking to my dad. "Is anything the matter? Is there something wrong with Dad?"

"No, no. Nothing's the matter with him."

Again I could detect a stiffness in the way she was speaking.

"I'm sure he'll reach you soon, so I think I'd better not say anything. He'll think I'm meddling."

Great. She had opened a door to a room, but left the light off inside. I was in the dark, for sure. We talked a bit more, then said goodbye.

Supper that night was turkey, with cranberries, mashed potatoes and gravy. I asked my uncle if they ate such big meals all the time, and he said, "Sure, got to keep the engine running, you know." His engine must be twice as large as most people's, because he had two helpings of everything.

When the meal was finished we sat awhile to — my aunt said — "let it all settle." My mashed potatoes had already found all the empty spots in my stomach by the time the phone rang again. A phone on the farm rings funny, two long and one short. The first time I heard it, I couldn't figure out why everyone just sat around, not answering. Finally my aunt jumped up and took the receiver from the wall.

"Hello?" she said with her usual cheeriness, but soon her voice had dropped and she sounded more serious. "Oh, yes. Hi, long time no hear. How're things? Uh-huh. That's good. Yes, she's right here." She put a hand over the mouthpiece and gestured to me. "Kim, it's your father."

I took the phone and sat down. Right away my aunt motioned for the others to move into the living room.

"Hi, Dad."

"Hi, kid. How's my favorite girl?"

He says that all the time, even though I am his *only* girl. I like it, though.

"Okay. I'm visiting Valerie and Jason. Oh, I guess you knew that or you wouldn't have phoned here."

"Hey, you're quick. Must be that fresh air. Are you having a good time?"

"Well . . ." I don't know why, but I couldn't tell him about the camera. And suddenly it seemed too complicated to tell him why I had been upset with Mom at first for taking me to the farm. Another thing, did he know about Al? If not, I would be going behind

Mom's back if I told him. While I paused, I had a shifting feeling inside that I was changing, that life for me was becoming tougher all the time.

At last I simply said, "Yeah, it's okay. We went horseback riding today and saw some falcons."

"Terrific. A real nature girl."

Another pause, this time from him. It occurred to me that we had not talked in several weeks. His voice sounded far away, as though it were stretched thin from the farm all the way to Ontario.

Then he came back on the line. "By the way, congratulations on your report card. I hear you improved in Socials and Math. Way to go!"

Report cards had come out a week earlier. The grades seemed ancient history to me, now that summer vacation was here. "Thanks," I said. I wanted to hold my dad, give him a real hard, long hug.

"Dad, I miss you. A lot."

"Hey, so do I." He cleared his throat. "You know I do."

"I can hardly wait for you to come out at the end of July, Dad. Maybe we can go to the Waterpark at West Edmonton Mall. We could get a day-long pass and go on the slides. I'll bet you're chicken to go on the Drop of Doom with me. My friend Carol says her dad's bald head started to grow hair after he went down it."

I expected him to laugh with me, but instead he sounded serious. "Uh, Kim, that's what I wanted to talk to you about. I won't be able to make it, after all. One of the managers in the company here changed his holidays, and they need somebody to be in the office while he's gone."

"But you promised!"

"I know, but there's no way I can get out of this."

"But, Dad, it's been Christmas since —" I will *not* — no, not, I repeated to myself — cry. My throat thickened and I swallowed several times, but not one tear fell.

"Honey, the other men have more seniority. I'm new with the company, and I more or less have to take what they give me."

Just like me, I thought. I have to take what you give me.

"I'm sorry — I really am."

His voice was low and I could hardly hear him.

"But look, Kim, I can get my holiday rescheduled for the end of August, I think. That way, we could still spend time together before school starts."

"Sure. Fine." If we didn't end this conversation soon, I *would* cry. How could he do this to me?

Soon we said our goodbyes and I hung up.

The house was very still. My relatives were in the living room, next to the kitchen, but nobody was talking. I guess they'd heard everything I'd said.

Jason appeared in the doorway. "Do you want to watch some TV?"

I shrugged and followed him into the living room. My uncle was holding a newspaper before him, and my aunt appeared to be studying a copy of *TV Guide*. Valerie was on the couch, her leg up on a stool. Everyone glanced at me as I entered the room.

"So, how's your dad?" my uncle asked.

"The same as ever," I replied, letting them figure that one out for themselves.

Jason switched on the television. He tuned in one of the three channels they get, and we watched something called "The BRAT Patrol." Trust him to still be interested in an old Disney program. Actually, it might not have been too bad. I can't honestly say. I don't remember very much of it. My mind was on other things.

CHAPTER ELEVEN

Have you ever seen a prairie thunderstorm? The crackling lightning and crashing thunder used to terrify me. I would stay away from the windows in our house and go downstairs to the basement, where we had a bathroom with no windows. There I would close the door and shiver with a comic book until the storm was over. A bad one still makes me nervous, but I can usually handle it now. That night, after my dad's phone call, there was a big storm.

The sky started to get dark while we were watching television. I dozed off on the couch but woke up at the first clap of thunder. Valerie was tired, too, so we both went upstairs to bed.

We sat on her bed, looking out the window at the bright stitching of light on the horizon. The rain was still some distance away, but moving in fast.

Valerie yawned. "The doctor gave me some pills to make my ankle quit hurting. He said they would make me drowsy. He's right." Stretching, she crawled under the covers and was asleep within minutes.

I sat up to watch the storm. Clouds dark and dangerous looking came sailing over the house, and the poplar trees in the yard whipped back and forth in the wind. Perched high in the house's second story, I imagined I was in a ship at sea, being tossed by a typhoon.

Flash. Probably high overhead, because the thunder came several seconds later. The yard and buildings leaped out to my eyes in a bluish white light. Another flash, then another. Soon the strikes were so close together that the room was as bright as day. Valerie slept through it all. Wow, those pills must be strong, I thought. Thunder rumbled and the windows of the old house rattled. My heart started to beat fast the way it did when I was a little kid, but I forced myself to stay at the window and watch.

After about an hour, the storm passed and it was quiet again. I opened the window for cooler air and realized that almost no rain had fallen. I lay on my cot, breathing deeply. For the second night in a row, I tossed and turned. But only for a short while. I fell into a deep sleep and had a very clear and powerful dream.

I was little again. Mom and Dad and I were in our old house, the one we lived in when we were still a family. They sat at the kitchen table, arguing about something.

Outside, a storm like the one I had just seen on the farm was breaking all around the house — only this time, it seemed to be hammering against the outside walls. Mom and Dad didn't appear to notice it.

I tried to get their attention. "Mommy, I'm scared."

She couldn't hear me, and I was so small, I could barely see up over the edge of the table. My dad just kept shaking his head at her, and he couldn't hear me, either.

"Mommy, Daddy — please!"

Crash! Lightning flashed, and the bluish light rushed through the kitchen. I fell, got up and ran to the basement. Before I went down the steps, I looked back at them one last time. They were both leaning forward over the table, yelling, but I couldn't hear what they were saying, because another crash of thunder shook the house.

There was a window at the end of the hallway, beside the basement stairs. It was open now, and just when another bolt of lightning crackled overhead, I saw a bird — a falcon — perched on the ledge. It raised its wing in a sweeping motion at me as if to say, "This way. You can get out this way. Hurry!"

But I shook my head at the bird. "No" I heard myself saying. "I can't. I'm afraid. That's where the storm is." And outside, in the eerie light of the storm, a man stood under a tree. He was the old man with a beard who had chased Jason and me. Nothing could make me go out there.

For some reason, I could not find the light switch for the stairs. I was afraid of the dark at the bottom, too, but not as afraid as I was of the storm. One step at a time, my hand on the wall, I went down. The last step was hidden by darkness, but I knew that the bathroom was to the left. I held my hands out in front of me, found the doorway and scooted through.

Slamming the door shut, I cowered in the pitch blackness. But something was wrong. The storm was in the house. I could hear it rumbling, banging on the floor above me. Under the door, the flashes of light got brighter and brighter. I began to cry.

Bang! Bang! The thunder was slamming the closed door! I was trapped, and it wanted in. Faintly, very faintly, I could hear my mom and dad calling out, "Kim,

Kim, honey, where are you?" But their voices were so far away.

The light got brighter and brighter, until I opened my eyes. It was early in the morning and the rising sun was pouring through the bedroom window. I hadn't pulled the drapes and Valerie's room faced east. Her bedside clock announced in red numbers that it was only 4:50 a.m.

I pulled the curtains and tried to go back to sleep. Val's breathing made a regular *ah, wheww*, pause, *ah, wheww*. And so on. A rooster crowed. A cow's moo somewhere echoed over the barnyard. A bird made a high *kee-kee-keeing* sound. My dream from that night kept coming back to me in bits and pieces. Sure, falling back to sleep would be easy.

I got up, dressed and went downstairs to pour myself a bowl of cereal. My aunt kept a notepad by the phone for messages, so I ripped off a sheet and scrawled, "Gone for a walk. Don't worry. (signed) Kim."

My dream was bugging me, making me feel crummy inside. Whenever I feel down that way, it helps me to go on a long walk.

Nobody else was up yet, not even my uncle. I crossed the empty yard and went around to the corral behind the barn.

Blackie and Madonna heard me and crowded up against the rails of the fence.

"Hey, I'd rather go for a ride this morning," I said, rubbing Blackie's nose, "but I could never get you saddled by myself."

Blackie licked me, covering my hand in a wet slobber.

"Sorry, no sugar, either."

I turned my steps to the open field. All my uncle's other fields had real crops growing, but this one seemed to be pasture, with only grass for the cows and horses. It was the same one we had ridden over the day before.

Maybe I actually knew where I was going without realizing it. After about ten minutes, I was obviously heading for the river. The sun was getting warmer. A small breeze ruffled the grasses. There was no sign of last night's violent storm anywhere in the bright blue sky.

I heard something behind me. Small, but getting bigger as I watched, was a horse with a rider — no, two horses with one rider. Light glinted on the rider's face. Glasses. It was Jason.

"Hey, you're up early!" he called as he pulled up beside me.

"So are you. Isn't Aunt Mary going to wonder where you are?"

"I read your note and added 'Me, too' to the bottom of it."

"Me Two Two? Are you sure your name isn't Jacob?" I teased.

He looked puzzled for a second, then his face creased in a grin. "Oh, yeah. The Hooded Fang. And the Dinosaur." He paused to glance in the direction I had been walking. "How about a ride?"

"Thanks." I took the reins to Madonna and mounted. The right way this time, without having to do a shuffle on the way up. Madonna snorted and backed up a few steps. "Maybe she doesn't want me to ride her," I said. She felt younger, more skittish than Blackie.

"We can trade if you like," answered Jason. "She should be good, though. Madonna, behave!"

Madonna stood still, waiting for my command. I had to hand it to Jason; he was good with animals. We set off at a walk.

"Were you going to the river?"

"Guess so. I didn't plan it that way, though."

"Maybe the old guy is still there. We can check to see what he's up to."

I had been thinking the same thing. "We'll have to be careful, though. If he sees us spying on him again, he'll probably tie us up and throw us in the river."

"I'd like to see him try." He stuck his chin out.

"He *is* a bit bigger than you, Jason. Size gives adults a certain advantage over us." As I said that, I remembered my conversation with my dad the night before, and a wave of anger swept over me. "That's why they get to make most of the rules."

Jason looked at me doubtfully. "Well, that's not the only reason."

I looked down at the saddle horn in front of me. Luckily my hair fell forward on either side of my head. Otherwise, Jason might have seen my eyes get watery.

"No, you're right. I guess they have good reasons for doing what they do," I admitted.

"Aren't you going to get to see your dad at all this summer?"

"Oh, yeah. He's coming out later than I thought, that's all. He did sort of break a promise to me, though."

A gopher poked his head from the ground off to my right. He whistled shrilly once before disappearing again.

"My dad breaks promises, too, sometimes," Jason added thoughtfully.

I could tell he was trying to make me feel better.

Yeah, I thought, but at least he's around to break them.

CHAPTER TWELVE

"He's still there. See his car?"

Jason pointed through the trees down the river ravine toward the bridge. A windshield glinted near the concrete pillars.

"Yeah. Are you certain you want to do this?" A few minutes earlier I had been all for sneaking another peek at the stranger, but now the memory of his anger at us in the Drum made me hesitate.

"We'll leave the horses here under the trees. He'll never hear us coming on foot."

Jason was already slipping off Blackie and leading the horse to a clump of poplar trees near the edge of the ravine. I followed his example and we tied the horses to a tree that had broken, its upper half lying on the ground.

We took the same easy slope down, but cut crossways to our right before reaching the bottom. When the ground leveled, we were only about fifty feet from the brown station wagon. In the clearing beside it, I recognized something. It made me feel suddenly foolish.

"Look, Jason. There's the canvas he bought."

He nodded. "You're right. And the rope, too."

Stretched between two trees was a canvas hammock, held up by the yellow rope we had seen the man carrying on the street. Yep, he was a mysterious and dangerous guy, this one. Probably spent his time in the hammock trying to figure out ways to take over the world — or, at the very least, how to smuggle falcons out of Canada.

"I feel dumb, Jason."

"Me, too."

I stepped into the clearing. Jason caught up to me and grabbed my elbow. "What do you think you're doing?" he whispered.

"We have to apologize," I said.

"Are you nuts? He'll probably eat us alive, anyway. Forget it, let's get out of here."

"No." I walked over to the tent and was about to open it, when a furious barking erupted from the side. I jumped, and a tiny dog — a chihuahua, I think — bounded into view at the end of a leash. He was tethered to one of the tent pegs, and he bounced up and down like a Ping-Pong ball.

"And this," I said, "must be who travels in the little cage."

I bent down and stretched out my hand. After a few more barks, the little dog sniffed my hand and licked it.

Just then there was a terrible commotion from the station wagon. We all jumped, and the dog started making a racket again.

"What's that?" Jason and I said together.

It came again, a banging, followed by what sounded like a human growl. Now I could see that the car itself was shaking violently.

"Do you have bears out here?" I asked. I looked around us nervously.

"No . . . at least, I'm pretty sure we don't. But once one of our neighbors said he had seen a wolf. And Mr. Tomkins a ways down the river said there was a cougar that —"

Thump. Thump. Bang. Bang. It sounded like some kind of monster was hatching in the back of the car.

Cautiously I circled around the edge of the clearing. The hammock swayed slightly as I ducked under it and peeked past a tree at the back of the car.

What I saw made my mouth drop open.

"Jason," I yelled. "Come here — quick!"

The station wagon tailgate was down. Two boots were visible, and above them, two ankles tied together with the same yellow rope used to suspend the hammock. While we stared, the bound ankles wriggled and the boots banged up and down on the tailgate. The weird growling sound came to us again.

"*Owlf*. Uf aye geg my hanns luff. *Arrr!*" *Bang, bang*.

We rushed to the car and saw the old stranger inside, his arms and legs trussed up and a gag over his mouth. Something wet and dark oozed from one side of his head. Blood. It took us a second to get over the surprise of seeing him that way. Jason asked me what we should do.

"Help me untie him." I began to crawl into the car.

Jason grabbed me from behind. "Who would have done this? And why?" he asked.

I knew what he was thinking. Here was the man who'd chased us down an alley, looking now as if *he* was a victim. It was confusing.

The man's face was all red, and his eyeballs were bulging, so I could see their whites quite clearly. When he turned his head, I noticed that the cut on his forehead continued to bleed. He was sweating and his shirt was soaking wet. He looked dangerous, but he also looked as though he was in pain.

"We can't leave him here," I answered, and crawled in to kneel by his side. "Take it easy," I told him. "We'll undo the ropes for you." He growled and shook once more, and I hesitated. "If," I added, "you promise not to hurt us."

He took a deep breath, sighed and nodded.

Luckily he must have been tied up while he lay on his back, because the knots were in front, making it easier for us to work on them. If the knots had been in back, we would have had to roll him over — and he was a large man.

When we had the ropes loosened, we helped him sit up. He reached around to get at the gag in his mouth, but groaned. Gently Jason and I slipped it up over the back of his head.

"Th-thanks. Say, aren't you the kids I tangled with in Drumheller yesterday? What's going on here? Are you a part of this — this outrage?" He glared at us.

Jason wriggled back and sat on the end of the tailgate. I could tell he disliked the old man and probably would never apologize. I had to do this alone.

"Uh, mister, I'm awfully sorry, but we made a terrible mistake yesterday. We thought — that is, we . . ." How could I explain this mess? Impossible.

"So, you aren't with those two men?"

I shook my head. "The ones who did this to you?"

He nodded. "Funniest thing, too. They didn't take my car or my wallet. Just tied me up and left me here. Almost as if . . ." His voice trailed off.

"How did it happen?"

"Hold on. My throat's dry." He stood, legs shaky, and poured some water from a jug beside the tent. Then he came back to sit beside us, drinking the water from a coffee mug. After taking two big swallows, he began.

"It was around four in the morning, after that big storm was over and a little before dawn. I remember being woken up by the sound of a truck or some vehicle passing nearby. It came down the ridge, then along the riverbank. I thought it was odd for anyone to be up and driving around that late or that early, however you look at it.

"I got up and followed in the same direction until I got to the place where the river widens out by the cliffs. I guess maybe you saw the place when you were here the other day, right?"

We nodded, and he continued.

"So, when I got opposite the cliffs, I saw

a truck all right, up behind me, but I saw something else that seemed peculiar. On the other side of the river were these two men, and they were getting ready to climb the cliffs. They had a rope and some other stuff slung over their shoulders. Now, I figured it was pretty strange for people to be hiking at that time of the day, so I decided to stay and watch."

He gulped the rest of the water from the cup, wiping his mouth with his sleeve. "Well, one of them happened to look around and he saw me. He stared, then said something to the other guy, who had already started up the cliff. The second one stared, then came back down. Then they both waded across the river to me."

They had seemed very nervous, he said, and demanded to know why he had been "spying" on them. That made him mad, they got into an argument and one of the men knocked him down, causing him to smack his head against a rock. After that they forced him to walk back to his camp, where they tied him up.

"What kinds of things were they carrying?" I cast an anxious look around us.

He shook his head. "Couldn't see much. But they both wore backpacks."

"Mr. — we don't even know your name. I'm Kim, and this is my cousin Jason."

"Mmph," he grunted. "Mine's Jack Rollins. Guess I should thank you for getting me loose."

"That's okay." I hurried on. "Mr. Rollins, I think those men are smugglers. There is a nest of rare peregrine falcons on that cliff, and someone — probably those men — has been stealing others in this area."

"Yeah? Well, I don't much care *what* they're up to. They can't get away with what they did to me is all I know." He reached into his pants, jiggling the pocket and making a tinkling noise. Taking out a set of keys, he staggered his way toward the car.

Alarmed, I followed him. "What are you doing?"

"Getting help. The police will settle these guys. And I know they haven't left, because their truck hasn't passed by again."

He took another step, but as soon as his foot touched the ground, he groaned and held his head. Swaying, he stumbled against the station wagon and sat down on the dirt.

Jason and I jumped to his side. His face was no longer red but white. Blood continued to trickle down the side.

"Mr. Rollins, you can't drive this way and you need a doctor. Can you wait while we ride back for help?"

His head tilted back, and he fell over.

Jason looked at me in horror. "Is he dead?"

I saw that the man's chest was heaving up and down regularly.

"No. He's passed out. But I think he needs a doctor. Fast. You'd better go, Jason."

"What about you? Do you really think you should be staying here alone? What if the men who did that come back?"

I glanced along the river's edge, to where it disappeared around the bend. "I think they're too busy with what they're doing to notice me. Someone should stay with him. I'll be fine — just hurry."

Jason stood wide-eyed for a moment before running to where we had left the horses. When he had gone, I went into the tent to find more water for Mr. Rollins. The sun was getting hot, even though my wristwatch read only 6:15 in the morning.

Mr. Rollins woke again and wanted to sit up. I helped him lean against the car tire. I said that Jason would get him a doctor, that everything was fine. At least, that was what I told him. I kept looking around, wondering if I would see two men come out of the bush.

CHAPTER THIRTEEN

Mr. Rollins moaned. His eyes fluttered, and he raised himself up on one elbow. "Thirsty," he muttered, and when I got the cup from beside the tent, he drank the rest of the water. The longer he stayed awake, the madder he got. He pounded the ground beside him with a fist.

"If I get my hands on those punks, I'll knock their heads together," he vowed.

He sounded like Jason when he talked like that, and I turned my head so he wouldn't see me smile. The thought of Jason old like Mr. Rollins and as grumpy as Mr. Rollins was very funny, indeed.

"Where's your brother?" he asked suddenly.

"He's my cousin. He went to get help for you."

"Ah, yes." He was thoughtful for a moment, then he turned to me excitedly. "And the police?"

"I suppose so." I sneaked another look at the cut on his head.

Mr. Rollins rolled to his knees and tried to get up. That scared me. I remembered reading somewhere that people with head injuries should not move. "You'd better stay still. You might be hurt worse than you think."

Sure enough, he put his hand to the side of his head and moaned before sinking to a sitting position. "But . . . those men . . . will get away. The police will be too late."

"No. No, they won't." I didn't even sound convincing to myself. They would have had enough time to get back to the cliffs and do whatever they wanted to do by now.

"Mr. Rollins, I'll go and see if they're still there. Will you be all right for a while?"

"Why, yes. But I can't let you do that alone. Those people are dangerous." He touched his wound again to remind me.

"I know, but I'll be careful. I won't get too close. They won't even see me."

He thought briefly, then nodded. "Stay on this side of the river. Watch that you keep behind cover."

I left the clearing, walking near the base of the ridge, where there were lots of bushes. I was glad that I'd worn jeans that morning, because the bushes had pointy twigs that grabbed at me. As I walked, I wondered where the men had parked the truck Mr. Rollins had heard. If they had driven along the top of the ravine, then they must have parked it somewhere near the trail Jason and I used to get down.

When I got to the trail, I looked up, and there, only a few feet from where Jason and I had passed, was a green pickup, parked between two trees. We had passed right by it and not even noticed! I saw it now, and I saw something else: the driver's side door had a rectangular sign on it — Protec. They were the two men who were doing tests for the oil company! Or at least that was what they claimed.

I crept through the last bit of bushes and trees, hunched over with my hands in front of my face. I could hear the gentle gurgling of the river, and soon saw the water itself and the cliffs beyond. And at the base of the cliff stood one of the men.

It was the older man, and he was waiting for his partner, who was climbing down with a bag slung over his shoulder. Above him the falcon nest appeared to be deserted, with no sign of either the parents or the young ones. I was convinced the fledglings were inside the bag.

The man lowered himself the last few feet until he stood on the sand. When he got to the bottom, he wiped his forehead with the back of his sleeve, taking off his sunglasses before he did.

That's when I recognized him! He was the man who hadn't gotten out of the Protec truck after it had almost run us off the road. And now I knew why. He was also Mr. Tessier's partner. A Fish and Wildlife officer was helping to smuggle the falcons.

Opening the bag ever so slightly, he let the other man peek inside and they grinned. He drew the string tightly again, and they looked both ways along the river. Then they stared straight across the water, directly at me!

I froze. I was behind leaves and the trunk of a small tree. I stopped breathing, thinking they would notice my chest moving. They turned their heads, though, as if they had not seen me.

After placing the bag gently on the ground, the men took off their hiking boots and slipped on knee-high rubbers. Then they began to wade across the water, taking careful strides. The man with the bag said something, laughing. The other man spoke sharply to him and I heard the word "Quiet!"

They came in my direction and hurried up the trail. I waited for a moment, torn between wanting to follow them and being too afraid to do so. Finally, when I thought they were far enough ahead, I climbed, too, being careful to stay as close as I could to the brush on the side.

Near the top, I sneaked diagonally across the hill to a point I thought was directly under the truck. Very carefully, on my hands and knees, I crawled the last distance up the hill. As I got near the crest, I heard voices.

"Take it easy! After all this, we want to make sure the product arrives in perfect condition."

"Okay. Hold the bag open while I slip these gloves back on."

"What about the old guy?"

"Nothing. We leave him where he is. By the time he gets loose, we'll be miles away from here."

"I dunno. What if he saw the truck?"

"Not a chance. He came along the water's edge. He never saw a thing."

They stopped talking and I heard something metal click. The sound was familiar somehow, but I was too far down to see what they were doing. I had to get closer.

The truck was right by the edge of the ravine. I raised myself over the low lip of grass and dirt and slithered to a back wheel. The truck itself was high, with big knobby tires, so I simply crawled underneath. I could hear myself breathe and my clothing rustle as I moved first one leg up, then the other. Finally I was in the middle, centered between all four tires.

The bag, brown canvas with metal rings and a thick string for drawing it together at the top, fell to the ground a few feet from my shoulder. It was empty now. Where were the birds?

One of the men spoke again. "There. I think that's got it."

"Be sure. Try the top again."

The other man grunted, and the whole truck swayed as if he were tugging on it.

"Hand me that wrench for a second," the first man said.

They shifted their feet slightly, and suddenly a wrench dropped to the ground and bounced to within inches of my nose. I began to do a crab crawl backward. One of the men kneeled and peered under the truck. It was Mr. Tessier's partner, the one I called Sunglasses.

He reached for the wrench and, as he did, looked sideways directly into my eyes! By this time I had scooted between the rear wheels.

"What — what are you doing —" he sputtered. "Hey, Nick, there's a kid under the truck!"

"Whaddya mean?"

The other man bent down, too, and they both stared. I stopped wriggling backward, too scared to do anything but stare back. For only a second, though, because now the men were coming to the rear of the truck. I scurried forward again, with a sudden crazy thought that I must be making a mess of my clothes.

One of them stayed on the passenger side of the truck while the other ran around to the driver's side. I was trapped, like a piece of baloney between two slices of bread.

The man on the driver's side was the one called Nick. He was the older man who had almost run us off the road the day Valerie, Jason and I went riding. He gave me a grim smile now.

"Well, well, we've met somewhere before, haven't we, miss?"

I felt the other man's fingers pluck at my runner. I gave a sharp kick and heard him yelp. Then he cursed me.

"Watch your language around our guest," Nick ordered Sunglasses. His voice became smooth as he said to me, "Come on out, we're not going to hurt you."

I felt like shouting "Liar!" in his face, but I realized that he didn't know how much I knew, such as the fact that I'd seen what they'd done to Mr. Rollins. I glanced away and saw again, lying beside the front tire, the brown canvas bag. It gave me an idea.

"I noticed the two of you coming across

the river, carrying the bag. You were acting kinda suspicious, so I decided to try to hear what you were doing." I deliberately left out any mention of the falcons.

Nick seemed to be thinking, then his face relaxed a little. "That's it? You saw us with a bag and you thought we were doing something wrong?" He propped his chin on his fist, as though we were friends lying around in someone's backyard, just goofing off and talking.

He chuckled. "If you promise not to run off, I'll show you something that just might lay your fears to rest."

He rose, and I could heard the door being opened. All I could see of him were his boots, big as a giant's.

When he dropped down once more, he was holding another canvas bag, similar to the first one. "You see," he said, opening the bag, "in a way, you were right. We were doing something wrong — but not illegal."

He tipped the bag up until several rocks about the size of my fist tumbled out. One rolled under the truck and I picked it up. It was gray and hard, just another rock.

"What's this?"

"A mineral sample," Nick explained patiently. "My partner and I are spies — for the oil company, that is. We're checking up on the competition to see what their reserves are like. There's no law against it, but if Foothills Oil finds out what we're up to, they'll be plenty mad."

I've heard about oil spies, so his story had just enough truth in it to be tempting — for somebody who didn't know that much about what oil companies can and can't do.

"Gee," I said, examining the rock, as if everything was suddenly clear, "is that all you guys were doing?"

"Uh-huh. Now, why don't you come out from under there?"

One thing was certain: whether I had fooled them or not, I couldn't squirm back and forth avoiding them all day. I scooted out on Nick's side.

"That's better." Nick helped me to my feet with a firm hand. Picking a twig from my hair, he said, "Sit down inside for a minute. We've got some cans of soft drink in the cooler in the back. You must be thirsty after making like a soldier there."

He was a strong man. He partially lifted me into the driver's seat and smiled. "Be right back." Then he disappeared, and I heard the door of the canopy opening. I looked over to the door mirror on the passenger side, and saw Nick step into view behind the back bumper, where Sunglasses was already standing.

Immediately they began to argue in

whispers. I could not hear them, but the younger man with the sunglasses was waving his arms, pointing in my direction. I didn't need to hear the words. I could read his lips as they clearly curled back to accuse me several times. "She's lying. She recognizes me!" He looked angry and very mean. I shivered. If I tried to run now, they would catch me easily. And then they would know for sure I was lying.

I glanced desperately around the inside of the truck. A map was folded neatly on the seat beside me. Otherwise the cab was bare. In the movies a gun is always conveniently forgotten by the kidnappers. Or at least a tool or weapon of some kind. I reached under the seat — and my fingers brushed a bulky, familiar object.

I tugged and out came my camera. I was holding it, when one of the men gave a surprised shout. I looked in the side-view mirror, where I saw them staring at me. No doubt they'd noticed I was holding the camera. As they began walking back to me, I desperately gave the cab one last once-over. That's when I spotted it.

The key was in the ignition. For half a heartbeat I thought, I'll just start the engine, turn this sucker around and drive to my uncle's place. I moaned. Oh, sure. As if I knew the first thing about driving. I'd seen adults do it all the time, but had never tried it once. Even that little pest Jason knew more about machinery than I did.

Or did he? The truck was parked with its nose pointed downhill at the river. I glanced at the gearshift lever. It was in Park. Then I checked the emergency brake pedal near the floor. It was pressed down.

I took a deep breath and muttered, "Kim, you are in a real mess," before pushing the gearshift into Neutral and twisting on a black handle labeled Brake. Immediately the truck began to roll forward.

In the rearview mirror, I saw the two men hesitate when they noticed the truck moving. Then, waving their arms and yelling, they began to rush forward. By that time it was too late. The truck picked up speed quickly, flattened a small bush and bounced over its first bump.

The truck was now going faster than a person could run — or so I thought.

Suddenly a hand reached out and grabbed the mirror on my door. Nick's face appeared beside it.

"You stupid kid, stop!" he shouted.

"I — I can't," I yelled back. It was true. I felt frozen, my hands glued to the steering wheel.

Nick was running hard, holding on to the mirror with one hand while trying to get the door open with the other. As he turned his head to look where we were going, his eyes widened. “Oh, no!” he hollered, before letting go and falling to the side.

I was headed straight for some trees. I tried to pull the wheel to the right, but it was locked in position. Mom, I remembered, once explained that happened if the ignition wasn't turned on, so I frantically fiddled with the key. I felt the wheel move, and pulled with all my weight.

I missed the first two trees, but hit the third one with the left headlight. There was a loud bang, and the truck shuddered before rolling on, scraping the tree along the driver's side. *Whack!* No more mirror on my door.

The truck jerked and bumped its way a little farther before getting wedged between two big poplars, just in front of the doors. Metal squealed as the fit got tighter and tighter. Then I felt the truck come to a complete stop.

I tried to open my door, but the first smack against the tree must have jammed the door, because it wouldn't budge. The passenger door was fine, though, and I threw that open and hit the ground at a run. I didn't realize, however, that the truck had stopped on the edge of a dropoff. I shot out over the edge and rolled down a slope.

I was traveling faster than I'd imagined. I tumbled through the grass and bushes, rolling over and over from my stomach to my back. Sticks poked me in the ribs, and I banged my elbow before finally coming to a halt against a small tree.

My elbow was numb and my right cheek felt funny, but I didn't have time to check myself out. The men were scrambling down the slope after me, hollering something that sounded like "Come back!" Fat chance. I stumbled, half rolled, then ran toward the river.

When I reached the water's edge, I looked back to see them still in the trees but approaching fast. Thankfully the river was so shallow and slow a person could almost run across. I took a shortcut across one bend, then used my track-and-field stride, kicking sand up behind me.

Have you ever tried to think when you're terrified? It's not easy. I ran as hard as I could, questions racing through my mind: Go to Mr. Rollins' car? Or go past it to the road? Mr. Rollins was in no shape to help, and if the men saw him out of the car, they might decide to kill him.

I churned around another bend in the river and sprinted toward the bridge. A glance backward told me the awful truth:

the men were gaining on me. They were fast, really fast runners!

I saw the edge of the clearing and the roof of Mr. Rollins' car. Now my pursuers were only about fifty feet behind me. I would have to cut through the clearing and make a desperate dash up the bank to the road. If I was lucky, a passing car would see me. If not . . .

I burst into the clearing, dodged the hammock, raced along the side of the car, rounded the back and — almost ran right into Jason.

And he wasn't alone.

CHAPTER FOURTEEN

The only other time I had seen so many different uniforms together was at a parade. Two ambulance workers were bending over Mr. Rollins, who was unconscious on the ground. A policeman was talking to Jason, while another officer stood next to them, listening. When I burst in on them, they all turned with a surprised look.

"Kim," Jason said, "what happened to you?" He reached up and touched my face, and I saw blood on his fingers when he took his hand away.

At first I couldn't speak I was so out of breath. A noise made us all turn around as Nick came stumbling into the clearing. He jerked to a stop, his eyes growing larger as he looked at all the people around me. His partner emerged, too, and would have turned right around again if Nick hadn't grabbed him.

Nick stepped forward. "Good," he said. "You held her for me."

Held me for them? What was he talking about?

"I don't want you to arrest her," he continued, " but this young lady stole my truck and very likely damaged it. I would like you to return her to her parents so she won't bother us any more."

I couldn't believe my ears. This jerk was in deep trouble himself, and he had the nerve to accuse me! It was a good thing Jason spoke up, because I'm sure my mouth was hanging open I was so amazed.

"Those are the men," Jason half whispered to the police officer.

The policeman crossed over to stand in front of Nick. "Were you involved in a fight with that man over there earlier today?"

Nick's eyes flickered to Mr. Rollins. The ambulance people were lifting him very gently onto a stretcher. That one glance told Nick that Mr. Rollins wasn't able to accuse him of anything at the moment.

He shook his head. "No. I've never laid eyes on him before. Have you?" he asked his partner.

The man in the sunglasses simply shrugged.

Nick asked the policeman, "Did he claim we hurt him?"

"No. He's obviously in no shape to talk."

"So, the kids are saying they saw us beat up the old man?"

"No, but they listened to him describe his attackers before he lost consciousness."

"I'm afraid, Officer, there's been a mistake here. These kids have let their imaginations —"

"He's lying," I broke in. "He beat up Mr. Rollins because Mr. Rollins saw them stealing the falcons. And I know where the birds are hidden — in their truck."

The first policeman turned to me. "So you saw the falcons?"

"Well, no, not exactly. But I know they must have —"

"This is ridiculous," Nick interrupted.

The two police officers stood looking at each other, and I could tell they read in each other's eyes the doubts they were both having. Nick's partner took his sunglasses from a pants pocket and put them on. His face away from the officers, he let a tiny smile curl his lips.

"Wait," I suddenly cried out. "There's something else! I just remembered — they have my camera. It was stolen from my cousins' house, and now they have it in their truck. They must be the ones who broke in and took it."

Mistake. Now the two officers looked totally baffled.

The first one, who was taking notes, bit on the end of his pencil. "There *was* a break-in over at the Schultz place yesterday. A camera was reported stolen. But now you —" he pointed the pencil at me "are saying these men stole the camera . . . *and* stole some birds . . . *and* attacked this other gentlemen." He stopped and blinked, as if the sun were too bright.

His partner simply stared at me.

"You see what I mean?" Nick raised his arms, appealing to the officers. "Isn't it all just a bit too wild? Look, tell you what. I'll even forget about the damage to my truck if you'll get these kids out of our hair. My partner and I have work to do, so we'll be running along now —"

"Not so fast," the RCMP officer interrupted. "Things are a bit confusing, but I think we can sort them out. We should start by checking your vehicle."

For a half a second, the smile vanished from Sunglasses, and Nick seemed ready to argue, but then he shrugged. "Okay, this way, if you think it's necessary."

After saying a few words to the ambulance people, the Mountie motioned for us to turn back along the river. I led the way, with Jason behind me, followed by Nick and his partner. The other patrolman was last.

It felt weird to be walking slowly along the same route I had so desperately run only minutes earlier. Everything was so peaceful now. The river moved slowly; the sun was already high above us. Then, breaking the silence, my stomach rumbled, and I remembered I'd eaten my bowl of cereal a long time ago.

"Is that the truck?" the officer behind Jason asked.

I looked into the trees, where the pickup had come to a halt tilted to one side. It had stopped almost at the water's edge, and the passenger door I'd escaped through hung open. "Yeah," I answered, not watching where I was going and stomping right into the water again. My Reeboks had taken a real beating the past few days: cow pies, dust and dirt, and lots of river dunkings. Mom would listen to my amazing story, but then she would shake her head and say, "Just look at those shoes!"

My shoes oozing water, I joined the others gathered around the truck as the police officer asked Nick, "Mind if we have a look inside?"

"No, go right ahead," Nick said with a shrug.

He tried to smile, but I could see he was faking it. There was sweat on his upper lip.

The Mountie leaned into the cab. "Did you say," he asked me over his shoulder, "that your camera was in here?"

I stepped up beside him. "It's right . . . here somewhere." The camera was not on the seat, or on the floor, or under the seat, either. I glanced around the bushes and the ground nearby. "It . . . it must have fallen out while the truck bounced around. Or maybe when I jumped clear and ran. They were chasing me and . . ."

Nick had his eyebrows raised, as if to say "I told you so."

"Never mind," the policeman said. "If it's anywhere in the vicinity, we'll find it." He backed out of the cab and straightened. "Now, about the birds."

The patrolman peered into the back of the truck and crawled inside. He moved things around, picking up instruments, cords and a briefcase. Each item received a careful examination, especially the map that was folded into a square.

Next the policeman got out and circled the truck to open the passenger door. He checked the glove compartment, on the seats and under them. I must have been dazed or light-headed, because I watched him without saying a thing. When he turned to look at me, puzzled, he asked, "You saw them take the birds?"

"Uh-huh, a bit farther upstream. They climbed the cliffs and used bags to put the birds in. Then they waded across and — Hey, look under the hood. They were doing something there. I bet that's where they put them!"

The officer lifted the hood, and Jason and I peered inside with him. Nothing. Just the usual jungle of wires and stuff. I was beginning to think I *had* imagined the whole thing, when just then we heard someone calling from farther down the river. Mr. Tessier stepped into view and walked quickly in our direction.

"Hello again," he greeted me when he'd joined us. "I hear you're in the middle of some excite —" His eyebrows arched, creasing his forehead, as he stared at the man with the sunglasses.

"Bob," he said, seeing his partner for the first time. "I thought you were in Calgary for the weekend. What are you doing here?"

Bob paused, then said, "I was helping my friend here do some surveying. There's no problem with what I do on my spare time, is there?"

"No," Mr. Tessier answered. "Not unless —"

"They took some young peregrines from a nest over there." I pointed. "And chased me because I saw them doing it."

Mr. Tessier listened intently, then looked hard at Nick and Bob. "Those are pretty serious accusations, Kim. You'd better fill me in on what's been happening here."

So I told him, but I was interrupted several times by Nick and his partner. When I'd finished, Nick noted sarcastically, "But you see, the mysterious camera is gone, and the two policemen here have searched the truck and found no trace of the supposedly abducted birds. I think this is all a case of confusion and good — but misguided — intentions."

Mr. Tessier ignored him. He kneeled beside the truck and asked one of the Mounties, "You checked it over closely?"

"We couldn't find anything."

Then he rolled onto his back and scooted under the truck. After crawling back out, he ran his hands behind the wheels, before reaching into the cab and pulling the seat loose. Next he stepped to the front of the truck. "Nothing in here, either, I take it?"

Then he reached inside and tried to move the lid on the air cleaner.

I knew what that was, because Mom had shown me once how to put in a new filter.

Suddenly I noticed something different.

"Hey —" I pointed excitedly " — there're *two* batteries!"

Mr. Tessier looked questioningly at Nick, who shrugged. "Sometimes when we know we're going to be out in the boonies for a while we put a camper on the back. It's standard to have a second battery, because you use more juice for lights and stuff."

Nick appeared fairly calm, but I had noticed Bob clenching his hands. He looked really tense. I stuck my face close up to the battery.

"Yeah," I said, "then why does this one have little holes drilled in the side, like air holes?"

There was a rapid movement behind me, and someone yelled. I looked to see Bob making a dash for the river, shoving aside anyone in his way. It was a dumb move, and he probably never would have made it anyhow, but we'll never know.

Bob knocked one cop over on his bum and was racing past me, when a foot appeared in his path. Jason was attached to the foot, and Bob was launched through the air to land face first at the shore. Instantly the two policemen had his hands behind him, with cuffs out and on.

When they had him on his feet and back by the truck, Mr. Tessier took his hand from

Nick's shoulder. "Not thinking of leaving us, are you?"

Nick's eyes were dazed as he shook his head.

"Let's see what's in here." Mr. Tessier had a jackknife out, and he pried at the top of the battery. The top popped loose and dropped to the ground. Inside, blinking at the bright light, were two young falcons, their feathers still a creamy color and fluffy.

"Jackpot!" he cried happily, putting his arm around my shoulder and giving me a big hug. "Kim, we should put you on the payroll — both of you!"

Jason was wearing a grin so wide his face seemed ready to split.

"Looks like they're none the worse for that rough ride down the hill," Mr. Tessier said, gently reaching in and lifting them out.

The peregrines craned their necks and began opening and closing their beaks.

"They're hungry already," he observed. "You people go on ahead. I should try to get these young ones back to their nest as soon as possible." He gave his former partner a withering look before grabbing some rope from the Protec truck and setting out across the river.

Jason and I wanted to help him, but the police officers asked us to come with them to make a statement.

As we headed back toward the bridge, I stooped to pick up something from the ground. "Oh, Bob," I said, holding up his sunglasses. "I think you dropped these."

Strange, he didn't say thanks when I slipped them into his shirt pocket.

CHAPTER FIFTEEN

"That nurse looked at you kinda funny."

We were walking down the corridor of the Drumheller Hospital, and Jason peered behind us in the direction of the admitting desk.

"Just act natural," I replied. Of course, I was having trouble doing that myself. Even though the temperature outside was above 30 degrees Celsius, I was wearing a jacket, zipped right up to my throat. Sweat trickled down my forehead.

There were four of us: besides Jason and me, Valerie, who limped only a little now, and Mr. Tessier.

"One twenty-three, 125. Here it is — 127," Jason read as we reached the bend in a hallway.

Mr. Tessier held the door open.

Mr. Rollins was propped up in his bed, white bandages covering the top of his head down to his eyebrows. "Well," he said as he saw us, "my rescuers. Come in, please."

We lined up beside the bed and asked how he was doing.

"Fine, fine, thank you. A bit of a headache," he added, touching the fresh white wrappings. "But, all things considered, not too bad. Hey," he said, pointing at me, "what's the matter with you?"

My jacket front was bulging and wriggling, and I couldn't keep myself from laughing. "Here," I said. "Someone wants to see you."

I unzipped the jacket and pulled out Mr. Rollins' dog. Immediately it began making swimming motions with its paws, trying to get to its master.

"José!" cried Mr. Rollins delightedly. "I was worried about you!"

I handed José over. "We hope you don't mind. We took him to the farm after the ambulance brought you here. If it's all right, we can look after him while you're getting better."

Mr. Rollins held the dog to his chest with one hand, running his other hand over the little animal's body. José squirmed and licked his face.

Jason watched, frowning, his arms crossed over his chest. "Why do you keep him in a cage? Isn't that kinda cruel?"

"Jason." Valerie's voice was low and warning.

For a moment, Mr. Rollins' eyes narrowed and I thought he would get angry the way he had before. But instead he smiled. "You just come right out and say what you think, don't you, young fella?"

Jason nodded once, his eyes darting to Valerie and me.

"I like that. Speaking your mind." Mr. Rollins massaged José's forehead gently with his thumb. "My friend here is still pretty young — a puppy, really. The cage is for traveling, mostly so he doesn't run around in the car. Or for around the camp when I can't keep an eye on him. He's almost outgrown it now." His face became serious. "I was pretty rough on you kids. Makes me feel kind of cheap right now. Forgive me?"

"Hey, no problem. We sort of jumped to conclusions, too. We thought you were —" Jason began to explain.

"Uh, that's okay," Valerie interrupted. "I'm sure Mr. Rollins is awfully tired after what happened to him." She shot her brother a look that said "Forget it already!"

Rollins rubbed noses with José. "It would take more than a crack on the noggin to keep a tough old bird like me down. Speaking of birds, whatever happened to the pair those characters took from the nest?"

"We put them back as soon as we could," Mr. Tessier said from behind me. "The parents were pretty upset, but looked as if they would accept the young ones back."

"What exactly were those those fellows up to, anyway?" Mr. Rollins asked.

Mr. Tessier explained to him about falcon smuggling, and how Nick and Bob had evidently been involved in the criminal operation for months. "And here I believed Bob was so dedicated — spending his free weekends out in the field, I thought, because he felt badly that we couldn't cover the area adequately." He shook his head. "He was in the best place to do the most damage."

We visited a short while longer, then I carefully put José back in my jacket. As we passed the reception desk on our way out, José let out a yelp. I bent over double to keep him from squirming loose, and the nurse on duty stared at me with wide eyes.

"If you're in pain, miss, we can take you right away in Emergency. Go straight through those doors and turn to your left."

When Mr. Tessier drove us back to the farm that evening, my aunt stuck her head out the back door and yelled, "Kim, your mom would like you to phone her as soon as possible. She's worried about you!"

I said I would, but wanted to take a second to thank Mr. Tessier for the ride. We shook hands, which felt a little weird, and then *he* thanked me for "solving" the falcon-smuggling case.

"Our department has been working on it for months now — the code name was Operation Falcon. But obviously Bob had us fooled. If it hadn't been for your alertness, they might have gotten away with it even longer."

"One thing," I asked, "why did they break into the house here and steal my camera?"

"Didn't you say you'd been taking pictures near the bridge? They must have thought you'd caught them in one of the photos. In the wrong hands, that could have been damaging evidence."

He thanked me again and started the engine. "Oh, by the way," he added, "do you think your mother will be coming out again soon?"

"I don't know. At the very least, she plans to pick me up a couple of weekends from now."

As the truck began to roll away, he added, "When you phone tonight, say hello to her from me."

After I got my mom on the phone, I explained everything that had happened and said I was fine, but she sounded worried, anyway.

"Still, Kim, I think I should be out there. You must have had a terrible scare. Besides, what if they haven't found all those crooks. You might be in danger and —"

"Mom, hold it. Believe me, everything's settled." Suddenly I had to laugh.

"What's so funny?"

"It's just what you always say about leaky faucets and flat tires. 'No problem, we'll fix it.' Everything's fixed, Mom. Relax, I'm okay."

There was a pause on the other end of the line. I could tell she was wondering, turning it over in her mind.

Quickly I added something else. "Mr. Tessier said to say hi to you."

"Who? Oh, that nice man in . . ."

"The uniform," I finished for her.

We both laughed.

We were near the end of the conversation, but I could tell there was one more thing bothering her.

"Kim, I'm sorry — that your father had to change his plans, I mean. I'm sure he couldn't help it. And I'm sure that in August he really will —"

"Mom," I broke in. "It's okay, really. If he comes out, it'll be great. And if he can't, well . . ." I paused. "Well, I can handle it."

When we hung up, I felt good. And I think she did, too.

Outside, I joined Valerie and Jason, who were sitting in the squeaky lawn swing but not swinging it. Twilight made everything seem softer, more peaceful. A few stars already twinkled above.

I settled in next to them and José, Mr. Rollins' dog, wagged his tail and licked my cheek. Then he whipped his head around to stare as a dark shape flew overhead. Wondering, I looked at my cousins.

"Probably an owl," explained Jason.

"Oh." I peered in the direction of the river. "Mr. Tessier said the falcons were doing fine, but I'd like to know for sure."

"We could take the horses out tomorrow morning," offered Jason. "And this time, we'll be careful not to climb so high."

"*Climb?!?*" Valerie and I glared at him.

Jason cringed and pulled his elbows close to his ribs, as if expecting to get jabbed. "Well, maybe not all of us. Maybe I could take the camera and sneak up without disturbing the birds and —"

Valerie nodded to me and we both stood up together. Then, grabbing the seat of the swing, we flipped Jason over backward onto the ground.

He felt around in the grass for his glasses and put them back on. Then he grinned up at us.

"I was only joking, you know," he said.

And he was, or at least he didn't try to climb the cliffs when we took pictures the next day. But for the rest of my stay at the farm, I was on guard for Jason's crazy stunts.

And checked every night for frogs in my bed.

ABOUT THE AUTHOR

Lyle Weis lives in Edmonton, where he is executive director of the Writers' Guild of Alberta. Before that, he taught English in elementary and high school, as well as at the University of Alberta.

In addition to *No Problem, We'll Fix It,* his first novel for young people, he has written many poems and short stories.

His two children, Erica and Jared, are an unending and delightful source of material for his work.